She'd Done Her Research—Long Before She'd Ever Even Met Him.

She'd read everything she could find about him. He was the brother who negotiated deals and wooed investors. The more she thought about it, the more she realized he wasn't really the black sheep of the family. No, he was the wolf in black sheep's clothing.

Definitely not the warm and responsive dad she'd choose for Isabella.

Emotionally unavailable, certainly. But cold? Maybe that wasn't quite the right word. Heat had shimmered in his gaze every time he'd looked at her. His touch had nearly scalded her. Passion seemed to lurk just beneath his surface, surging forward at every reminder of the night they'd spent together.

Except *they* hadn't spent a night together.

They had never met before twenty-four hours ago.

Dear Reader,

What woman can resist the lure of diamonds? Certainly not me! They're symbols of glamour, wealth and—of course—love.

That's why, when I decided to work on stories about two brothers, I decided they should own a diamond mine in Canada. Dex Messina is my kind of hero—a rich and powerful confirmed bachelor who is about to meet his match. Toss in a determined heroine, a charming imp of a baby, a few of those beautiful diamonds and just a hint of Cinderella, and you've got a story I just loved writing!

I hope you enjoy it, too. Look for his brother Derek's story in October 2008.

Enjoy!

Emily McKay

EMILY McKAY

BABY ON THE BILLIONAIRE'S DOORSTEP

Published by Silhouette Books
America's Publisher of Contemporary Romance

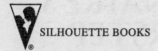

SILHOUETTE BOOKS

ISBN-13: 978-0-373-76866-0
ISBN-10:   0-373-76866-4

BABY ON THE BILLIONAIRE'S DOORSTEP

Visit Silhouette Books at www.eHarlequin.com

Printed in U.S.A.

Books by Emily McKay

Silhouette Desire

Surrogate and Wife #1710
Baby on the Billionaire's Doorstep #1866

EMILY McKAY

has wanted to write romance novels since she read her first Harlequin book when she was eleven. Now that she's all grown up, she still thinks it's the best job in the world!

Despite all the Harlequin Presents books she read during those formative years, she did not grow up to marry a Greek shipping tycoon, but rather her college sweetheart, who turned out to be the perfect romance hero. They live in Texas with their little girl, two big dogs and one beleaguered cat.

When she's not writing (or reading), she likes to garden, bake and hear from fans. You can contact her at Emily@emilymckay.com.

To my partner in crime, Robyn DeHart. My dear friend, without your help I'd be unable to write a book. Without your friendship, I probably wouldn't want to.

One

As the taxi pulled to a stop in front of the sprawling monstrosity his brother called home, Dex Messina pinched the bridge of his nose. Man, he was tired.

He was getting too old for this. He'd just spent a week in Antwerp working sixteen-hour days getting ready for the opening of Messina Diamonds' new diamond-cutting branch. On top of that, the seventeen-hour flight from Belgium—complete with a six-hour delay in New York—had taken its toll.

"This the place?" the cabbie asked from the front seat.

"Home sweet home."

Since the renovations on his own urban loft had hit yet another snag, Dex was living with his brother, Derek, a situation that suited neither of them and had been going on far too long. Only the amount of time Dex spent out of the country and the fact that he stayed in the detached guesthouse made it bearable.

Dex handed the driver a fifty, pulled his bag from the seat beside him and climbed out of the car. He swung the rugged canvas duffel over his shoulder and walked up the curved path. The towering oaks and clusters of shrubbery were perfectly manicured to hide the house from the road while creating the impression one had left the exclusive Dallas neighborhood of Highland Park altogether.

Ivy crept up the far corner of the building. A low stone retaining wall crumbled at one end. Both gave the impression of gently declining nobility.

Everything in Derek's life was like that. Perfect. Controlled. Pretentious.

It set Dex's teeth on edge. Made him want to take his motorcycle out of storage and pop some wheelies on his brother's plush green lawn.

Not that he would. He was a respectable contributor to the family business these days. A damn pillar of society.

Why he even—

Dex stopped short just shy of the mahogany double doors.

"What the—"

He stared for a long moment at the object blocking his path before he convinced himself he wasn't hallucinating.

It was an infant car seat.

Next to the car seat sat a bag decorated with smiling cartoon bears. Far more disturbing than the car seat itself was what appeared to be in it. A pile of blankets, out of the top of which rose a tiny pink stocking cap.

Dex crouched down to get a closer look, then thought better of it. Instead, he yanked his cell phone out of his pocket and dialed his brother's number.

"Derek here."

"You at home?"

"Yes. Don't tell me you missed your flight. I need you in the office to—"

"No. I'm at the front door. You might want to join me."

"Then why are you calling me?" A note of frustration crept into Derek's voice.

Dex was too shocked to be annoyed by it. "Just get your butt down here."

He flipped his phone closed. Sitting back on his heels, he rubbed his hand along his jaw, staring at the car seat and its bundle of…joy or whatever.

Five minutes later Derek swung open the front door. He had clearly been working. He'd lost his jacket and tie and the sleeves of his white dress shirt were rolled up. "This better be good."

Dex said nothing but looked up at his brother with a quirked eyebrow, waiting for Derek's reaction. If he hadn't been so completely thrown for a loop himself, the situation might have been amusing.

Derek looked down at the car seat. "Is this some kind of joke?"

"If it is, I'm not in on it."

"You didn't bring this thing home with you?"

Dex chuckled despite himself. "No. I didn't bring home a baby from Antwerp. I'm guessing that would be illegal."

"What's it doing here?"

"It was here when I drove up." Feigning a flippancy he didn't quite feel, Dex reached into the car seat and pulled aside the blanket to reveal the tiny head of a sleeping infant. The baby's skin seemed impossibly pale in the moonlight, its delicate rosebud of a mouth the only color in its face.

The infant was so still, he couldn't even tell if it was breathing. Feeling a burst of panic, he pulled loose the pink blanket and pressed his palm to the tiny cotton-covered chest.

The infant drew in one shuddering breath, then exhaled slowly. As he felt the warm breath drift across his hand, he felt something tighten inside of him, even as relief rocked him back on his heels.

"It's alive?" Derek asked.

"Thank God."

"What's that?" Derek asked.

Dex looked to where Derek was pointing. When he'd untucked the blanket, he'd dislodged a note. He picked it up and stood.

Derek took it from him and stepped out of the shadow of the doorway so that the landscape lighting from the yard shone on the note.

> D—
> Her name is Isabella. She's yours. You'll have to take her for a while.

The note wasn't signed.

For a long moment, Derek and Dex merely stared at each other. Then they both turned to stare at the baby.

"This is quite the mess you've gotten into this time." There was a note of grim censure in Derek's voice.

"*I've* gotten into?" Why it surprised him that Derek assumed this was his mess, he didn't know. "Who says it's mine?"

Derek propped his hands on his hips. "It's not my baby. I'm scrupulously careful about that kind of thing."

"Trust me. About that kind of thing, so am I."

"You found her," Derek pointed out.

"Yes. At *your* house."

"Where we both live."

They stared each other down, neither relenting.

Even as he looked into his brother's steely-blue eyes, Dex knew how ridiculous the conversation was. Yet conceding that they had no way of knowing who'd fathered the baby was like admitting that it could be his.

A little mewing sound came from the car seat and they both turned to the baby. She moved her head, her mouth opening and closing as if searching for something. He'd been on enough flights with crying babies to know that this could go very bad if they didn't do the right thing.

He dropped to his knees, ran his hand along the edge of the car seat and found a pacifier attached by a cord. With the precision of a movie hero disarming a nuclear weapon, he eased the pacifier into her mouth.

Holding his breath, he watched her suck contentedly, bringing a hand to rub against her cheek and then fall back asleep.

From behind him, Derek let out an audible sigh. "This is ridiculous."

Pulling his phone out of his pants pocket he spoke into the phone. "Call Lorraina."

"You're calling Raina?" Dex asked in a whisper as he pulled Derek farther away from the baby. "It's after midnight on a Sunday night."

"So?"

"It's a little late to be calling your assistant. Besides, someone abandoned a baby on your doorstep. We should call the police."

Derek's gaze narrowed. "Absolutely not. That would be a public relations nightmare."

"And naturally the public image of Messina Diamonds is more important than the welfare of this baby."

He didn't know if Derek heard him or not because by then Raina had picked up and Derek was talking to her. A few minutes later, he flipped his phone closed. He stood, hands clasped behind his back, glaring at the tiny infant.

"She said she can't come."

"I can't blame her."

"She did give me some…advice." Derek sounded disgusted. "She said if the baby wakes up, we should feed her."

"Then I guess we're on our own."

Dex stared at the car seat before mustering the courage to approach again. Derek, he noticed, didn't seem any more eager than he was to move the child off their front door step and into the house.

Finally, Dex pushed himself forward, plucked the car seat up by the handle and headed inside. Derek stopped him before he reached the door.

"Do you think that's wise?"

"She's a baby. Not a vampire. We've got to bring her into the house at some point."

Derek nodded reluctantly and followed them into the front room. Dex set the car seat down in the shadow of the sofa, where the lights wouldn't shine on her face, then sat down in the chair beside her to wait.

Derek handed him a brandy before lowering himself to the armchair opposite. "You'll have to stay with her tomorrow."

Dex nearly choked on the brandy. "Why me?"

"I leave for London at noon."

"Why can't Raina watch her?"

"Raina's coming with me. She'll be back by the end of the week, but she's going to be busy planning the reception for next week. You'll have to find someone to watch the child soon. Someone you can trust. I need you in the office by Tuesday for the board meeting."

Dex took another sip of his brandy. "Good thing you're not leaving until noon."

Derek looked up. "Why's that?"

"Because first thing in the morning, we're going to go get paternity tests."

Lucy Alwin—as a rule—didn't lie. She didn't like doing it and she wasn't any good at it.

But today, she was going to have to lie her butt off. And she'd better damn well be convincing at it. Isabella's future was at stake.

She double-checked the address one last time and turned her Toyota Prius onto Briarwood Lane. The sight of one mansion after another did little to quell her nerves and only reinforced what she already knew. The Messinas were filthy rich. And very powerful.

She eased her car to a stop across the street from number 122, mentally cursing her twin sister yet again. She'd warned Jewel a year ago, "You have to tell Dex Messina you're pregnant now. He needs to know he's going to be a father. Because if he finds out later that you've deceived him, he may do everything in his power to take your baby away from you."

But had Jewel followed her advice? No. Instead, she'd been determined to do this her own way. And on her own. Of course, Jewel's definition of "on her own" involved relying heavily on Lucy. From the moment she'd first held her darling niece in her arms Lucy hadn't minded one bit.

But over the past month, Jewel had slowly been withdrawing from both Lucy and Isabella. Then, late last night— long after Lucy was asleep—she'd dropped sweet baby Isabella on Dex's doorstep, then hightailed it out of town.

It was morning before Lucy had even realized they were

gone. Jewel, apparently in an attempt to reassure Lucy, had left a note saying she was going out of town for a couple of weeks, but that Lucy shouldn't worry, she'd left Isabella someplace safe.

For the first time in her life, Lucy was thankful for her sister's laziness. Jewel hadn't bothered to move Isabella's car seat from Lucy's car to her own. Instead she'd borrowed Lucy's Prius only to exchange it later on her way out of town for her own car. Thank God she had. Jewel had used the car's GPS system to look up Dex's address. That was the only way Lucy had known where Jewel had left Isabella.

It had taken Lucy another three hours to design and execute a plan to get Isabella back. A plan that involved raiding her sister's closet and having her hair cut and dyed to match Jewel's vibrant red.

In short, Lucy had to convince Dex that she was Isabella's mom and that she'd made a terrible mistake abandoning her baby. To do that she'd have to first convince him she was the woman he'd had a one-night stand with fourteen months ago.

How exactly she was going to do that was the question that had plagued Lucy since she'd developed this hare-brained plan. She and Jewel didn't just dress differently.

Lucy was sensible, no-nonsense practicality while Jewel was exotic, seductive sexuality. In short, Jewel had a way of manipulating and controlling men that Lucy had never comprehended, let alone replicated.

If Dex remembered Jewel at all—and men never forgot a woman like Jewel—then Lucy was going to have a hell of time convincing him that she was her twin sister. Her best hope was to get in and out of there as quickly as possible and pray that he wouldn't look too closely at her.

She didn't know if she could pull this off. She only knew she had to try. For Isabella's sake.

The Messinas, for all their wealth and privilege, were known for their ruthlessness. For their cold-hearted pursuit of the all-mighty dollar. No way Lucy was going to let one of those men care for her niece.

No, Isabella needed someone in her life who would always do the right thing for her. Since that person obviously wasn't going to be Jewel, Lucy was more than happy to step up to the plate.

With that thought spurring her on, Lucy stalked up the winding front path and rang the doorbell. She heard Isabella's cries from the behind the door and distress clutched her throat. Any lie she told today was well worth it.

She had to remind herself of that when the massive front door swung open to reveal Dex Messina, looking just as attractive as he had the first time she'd seen him, but considerably more rumpled and annoyed.

"Are you the nanny?" he asked.

"No. I'm the mother."

Two

Dex hadn't realized a baby could scream so loudly. Or for so long.

The baby had started crying the minute he'd been left alone with her and hadn't stopped nearly ninety minutes later.

Convinced her piercing cries had destroyed his hearing, he thought he'd misheard the woman at the door. "You're the what?"

"The mother," she repeated. "I'm Isabella's mother."

Isabella chose that instant to stop crying, so this time, Dex had no trouble hearing the woman. Instinctually, he brought up his arm to block the door as he studied her. But maybe Isabella was just catching her breath because, after a moment, she let out another bloodcurdling scream.

The woman rose onto her toes—for all the good it did her—trying to see Isabella over his shoulder. She bobbed first to one side, and then the other. Then, with unexpected speed and grace, she darted under his arm and into the house.

She dashed through the foyer to the living room with what he could only assume were a mother's instincts, straight to the car seat where he'd deposited the crying Isabella when the doorbell rang.

She scooped up the baby, held her at arm's length for a moment as if assessing the damage, and then cradled her close. The woman crooned softly to the child, swaying back and forth. Instantly the cries stopped.

In the blessed silence that followed, Dex's ears continued to ring. Hours of listening to Isabella cry had left his head throbbing and his thoughts muddled. And despite all that, the woman looked familiar.

She was dressed in a denim miniskirt and a pink tank top that barely covered her generous curves. Her pale, heart-shaped face was dusted with freckles. Her garishly red hair cut into a wedged bob.

It was the hair he remembered first. That and her hips. There was something sensuous in the way they shifted from side to side as she swayed. Something deeply erotic that pulled at him on an instinctual level.

Pick up the beat a little and add in the heavy throbbing bass from the bar and he'd think he was having a flashback to…when was that? A year ago? Longer?

His father had just died. There'd been the funeral followed by endless meetings and conferences divvying up the estate and business. Within a week, he'd been sick to death of death. Ready to lose himself in a bottle of Scotch and a warm, willing body.

He vaguely remembered that night. Had she been that body he'd lost himself in?

It was exactly the kind of relationship at which he excelled. No emotion. No future. No commitment.

But apparently something had gone terribly wrong.

* * *

Lucy kept waiting for Dex to say something. Anything.

Instead, he just watched her. His face inscrutable, but the tension evident in every line of his body.

With every minute that passed, her own apprehension grew. Finally, in a burst of defiant anxiety, she blurted out, "I made a mistake."

He lifted one eyebrow in silent, sardonic question.

"Okay, a big mistake. Huge really."

"You abandoned your baby on my doorstep. That's more than a mistake."

"But—" she held up her index finger to emphasize her point "—I realized it was a mistake, and I came back for her." Her heart was pounding and her nerves loosened her tongue. "So no harm done, right? And since you obviously don't want her, I'll just pack her up and we'll be on our way. You'll never hear from us again."

Holding her breath, she clutched Isabella tightly in one arm, swooped up the car seat in the other, and dashed for the door. For an instant, she even hoped it would be that simple.

But of course, it wasn't.

He grabbed her arm as she strode past, pulling her to a stop. His grip on her arm was almost painfully firm.

"Is she mine?"

Damn it. Why couldn't she be the kind of woman who would lie about this sort of thing? But, for better or worse, she wasn't.

When she hesitated, he continued. "In two weeks I'll have the results from the paternity test. I'll know for sure then."

"Two weeks?" she asked, her heart constricting at the thought of what might happen at the end of those weeks.

"Yes. Two weeks. That's how long the results will take since Derek and I both sent in samples to be considered. Apparently it takes that long when the possible fathers are brothers."

"I wasn't surprised at how long it would take. I was surprised you'd already done the test. Didn't take you long. Eager to dodge the bullet of fatherhood, aren't you?"

"Is she mine or isn't she?"

"She's yours."

"Then why did you hesitate?"

"I thought if you didn't know she was yours, you might just let us go."

"Even if she wasn't mine, you abandoned her."

Lucy hadn't counted on this.

In fact, she'd been so sure Dex would be so eager to get rid of Isabella, that he wouldn't think twice about handing her over.

Anger and frustration welled up inside her as she clutched Isabella even tighter. She blinked back tears, held Isabella even more tightly and made the only argument that had even a chance of winning him over.

"You can't possibly want to keep her yourself. Even if she is yours."

"Whether or not I want her is irrelevant. There's a reason abandoning a child is illegal. You're obviously not a fit parent."

And yet he hadn't called the police. That was something, wasn't it?

Knowing she couldn't possibly win an argument about whether or not she was a fit parent, she turned the tables on him. "No offense, but by the sound of things when I got here, it didn't seem like you were doing much better."

His eyes narrowed. "You're right, I don't want a baby. But if she really is mine, then I don't have a choice. To be honest, I don't have the faintest idea what to do with her. But you obviously do."

"I'm her mother," she insisted. "Of course I know what to do." And for a moment, she imagined she still might get out of this. But first she'd have to convince him he really could trust her with Isabella. But how could she do that when every cell of her body abhorred what Jewel had done?

As inconceivable as Jewel's actions were, Lucy tried to imagine what could possibly have been going through her sister's mind last night. Still swaying with Isabella in her arms, she gazed up at him, letting all her love for Isabella show in her eyes.

"The truth is, being a single mother is harder than I thought. But I've been doing this for five months now. After all that time, I had one night—just one night— when I got freaked out and felt like I couldn't do it anymore. Leaving her on your doorstep was stupid, but surely every parent is allowed one mistake. Even if it's a big one."

She held her breath, waiting for his response. If he didn't let her leave with Isabella now, she didn't know what she would do.

Finally, he responded. "You're right. I'm clearly not equipped to take care of an infant. But there's no way I'm handing her over to you, either. However, since the nanny service I called this morning appears incapable of sending someone over in a timely manner, you can stay here with the baby until I find someone suitable to watch her."

Before she could even feel relief, he pinned her with another of his cold stares.

"Just remember this is temporary. And I'm not letting you out of my sight."

* * *

Thirty minutes later, Lucy steered her car onto the Dallas tollway toward her condo. Normally she was a fairly calm driver—if perhaps overly cautious. But who wouldn't be in her profession? After all, she spent her days crunching numbers, calculating the odds of a person dying in a fiery car crash. In general, actuaries were very safe drivers. Today, however, she was a nervous wreck.

No doubt it had something to do with the fact that Dex was seated beside her. Since she and Isabella were going to be living in his house for at least the next few days, they needed clothes, formula, diapers…the gazillion things an infant needed. When she'd pointed this out to Dex, his first reaction had been to call the local baby superstore and have one of everything delivered. She'd quickly vetoed that idea.

No, if they were going through with this ridiculous plan, then Lucy wanted to retain what little control she had. And the very last thing she wanted was to make any of this easier on Dex. She certainly wasn't going to help him outfit a nursery for Isabella at his house. At the end of the two weeks—if not before—she intended to walk out of his life, taking Isabella and all of her stuff with her.

As she navigated the busy Dallas traffic, she kept up a constant mental litany of reasons why he should trust her with Isabella.

The second he'd gotten into the car, he'd shoved the seat back as far as it could go, stretched his denim-covered legs out in front of him, tipped his head back and closed his eyes. Unless she was mistaken, he'd fallen asleep. Probably taking advantage of the few blessed minutes of silence.

She remembered all too well the few nights she'd been up all night long with Isabella. They were as frustrating as they were exhausting.

Perhaps fatigue explained his behavior so far, which had ranged from rude to suspicious to downright insulting. Or perhaps he just thought she had it coming, after abandoning Isabella on his doorstep. But she couldn't feel sorry for Dex, despite what Jewel had put him through in the past twenty-four hours. Her first concern had to be Isabella's welfare.

Before showing up at his house, only two possible scenarios had occurred to her. Either he would have immediately contacted child protective services or he would have been so eager to get rid of Isabella, he wouldn't have questioned Lucy when she came to take her off his hands.

She'd never considered the possibility that he wouldn't want to give up the baby.

After all, from what she knew about Dex Messina, he was the jet set, playboy, black sheep of the Messina family.

As soon as she'd found out Jewel was pregnant with his child, Lucy had given in to her curiosity and run a Google search him. As wealthy and powerful as the Messina family was, it wasn't hard to find information about him.

What she'd learned had only been confirmed this morning when she'd met him in person. He was surly, unapproachable and…just difficult. More importantly, he didn't want to be a father. His rush to take the paternity test proved that, didn't it? And how could she help but resent being accused of being irresponsible by a man with Dex's reputation?

By the time she pulled her car into the spot outside her condo, she was practically fuming.

No one loved Isabella like she did. She was the best person to care for her. She knew it in her heart. Now, she just had to convince Dex.

Three

"Is all this really necessary?" Dex eyed the growing pile of baby accoutrements, which had begun to collect by the door.

"Babies need a lot of things," she called from the upstairs bedroom. "This is why I didn't want you to buy all new things."

Isabella—no doubt exhausted from her earlier rampage—lay asleep in her car seat on the living room floor.

The woman—and, damn it, why couldn't he remember her name?—emerged from the stairs carrying a suitcase. She dropped it by the door and immediately moved on to the kitchen. She'd changed from the miniskirt and heels into jeans and white Keds, a combination that took her skimpy pink tank top from tawdry to tomboy. The effect was oddly appealing in its wholesomeness. He half expected her to pull a baseball glove out of her back pocket and suggest they toss a few around in the backyard, or maybe offer him a slice of apple pie and a glass of lemonade.

Dex followed her into the kitchen, propped his shoulder against the doorway and watched as she moved about the tiny room.

She wasn't the sort of woman whose company he normally sought out. Despite the bright hair, there was nothing exotic about her. Nothing overtly sexual and enticing. Nothing flamboyant. Nothing that screamed, "For a good time, call…"

Instead, there was an efficiency about her, a sort of no-frills, no-nonsense simplicity that made her a pleasure to watch.

It wasn't that he was only attracted to party-girl bimbos. But he wasn't a long-term relationship kind of guy. He traveled a lot and didn't have the time or energy to devote to relationships. When he was in the country, his business commitments kept him busy enough without adding a needy girlfriend into the mix.

So how had he ended up sleeping with… "Damn it, what is your name?"

She looked up, her eyes wide and startled. "Lucy." Then she looked back down to frantically dig through the cupboard. "I mean, my legal name is Jewel. But I go by Lucy. Lucy Alwin."

She dropped a handful of plastic baby bottles into a paper grocery sack and rubbed her palms on her jeans.

"I make you nervous."

She started to lick her lips, but seemed to realize that only proved his point and pressed them firmly together. "Yes, you do."

"Why?"

She giggled. "You have to ask? You hold the fate of my child in your hands."

"Our child," he corrected. As he said the words, he felt something shift deep inside him.

That infant in the other room—the one who had frustrated and annoyed him so, who had thrown his life into upheaval—had been created when he'd had sex with this woman. When he'd stripped off her clothes, caressed her skin and plunged his seed deep into her body.

Almost as if she could read his thoughts, Lucy's eyes grew wider and she took a step backward. Her chest was rising and falling rapidly and the movement drew his gaze to the soft curve of her breasts.

He willed himself to remember what her breasts looked like, how they'd felt in his palms, but the memory didn't surface.

It had been so long ago. His memories of her were just snatches. Her enticing smile, the sway of her hips, the taste of tequila on her breath.

None of those images jived with the woman standing before him.

Maybe it was the way her simple jeans and tank top minimized the luscious curves of her body without hiding them. Or maybe it was the way she'd rocked Isabella in her arms, the very icon of maternity. Or the way she smelled faintly of baby powder.

Combined, they made her seem so wholesome. Almost innocent.

He might even buy it, if he hadn't picked her up in a bar and slept with her.

But because he had, he couldn't help wondering what it would be like to do so again. Without the liquor this time. With his senses fully intact. And he couldn't think of a damn reason not to.

Other than the fact that she'd already deceived him. She may not have lied outright, but wasn't having his child without telling him the worst lie of omission? But of course, sleeping with her and trusting her weren't the same thing at all.

He smiled wickedly at her. "I do hold your fate in my hands. You should remember that."

Part of him expected her to balk or shy away from him. Instead, she bumped her chin up and met his gaze straight on.

"Yes, you do. But that doesn't mean I'm going to let you bully me."

"Bully you?"

"Don't pretend you don't know what I'm talking about." She faced him with her hands on her hips. There was the faintest tremble in her voice, but he could tell she struggled to control it. "There you are, looming in my kitchen doorway, leering at me like the big bad wolf, ready to gobble me up if I make one wrong move."

He closed the distance between them. "If I'm the big bad wolf, what does that make you?" He tweaked a lock of bright red hair. "Little red riding hood?"

She swatted his hand away and narrowed her gaze at him. "Just remember how that story ended. Little Red Riding Hood learned her lesson and the wolf came to a bad end."

"Don't worry, red. I have no doubt you know how to take care of yourself. You've done a bang-up job so far."

"What's that supposed to mean?"

"The elaborate show of maternal care. The wide-eyed innocence. The sorrowful regret for your mistakes. It's all very touching. But don't think for a minute I've fallen for it."

"All very touching?" The pitch of her voice rose sharply and her chin bumped up another notch.

She stepped closer to him, hands still propped on her hips defiantly as she got right in his face. Or as close to his face as she could get, considering she had to be close to a foot shorter than him.

"You think I'm somehow faking my emotions? That my concern for Isabella, that my regret, is somehow planned? Is part of some scheme? Why would I do that? What could I possibly hope to achieve?"

"I don't know. You tell me."

For a moment, her mouth opened and closed rapidly, like a fish gaping in the air. Then she snapped it closed and shook her head. "What kind of person do you think I am?"

He stared down into her green eyes and felt bitter anger coil through his gut.

"I think you're the kind of woman to have a baby without letting the father know it's his."

Her face went white, then she threw up her hands in frustration as she turned away from him. "Well, that's hardly my fault."

He grabbed her arm and spun her back around to face him, surprised by his sudden burst of anger and looking for a way to vent it. "Then whose fault is it?"

She pressed her hands into his chest, trying to wedge some room between them, but he didn't release his hold on her. "This is the twenty-first century. It's gauche to blame a woman for getting pregnant. Not to mention ignorant. We're both responsible for what happened that night."

"I'm not talking about what happened that night. I'm talking about your decision afterward not to tell me you were pregnant."

"Funny, I don't recall us exchanging phone numbers before we parted ways. Maybe you should make a note of that for the next time you decide to pick up a woman in a bar."

The words "pick up a woman in a bar" were said with more than a hint of scorn. As well as a healthy dose of indignation. As if she were an innocent bystander to this train wreck.

"Don't make me into the villain here."

"Then don't me make into the villainess." She tugged again at her arm and this time he let her pull herself free. "I made a decision. I thought it was the right one at the time. You're not exactly a model of upstanding responsibility. It never occurred to me that you'd *want* to know you were going to be a father."

And until this moment, it hadn't occurred to him, either. Hell, he still wasn't sure he *wanted* to be a father. That was an issue that was going to take a lot more than just one day to get used to.

But he did know this: given the choice of having a five-month-old baby sprung on him versus having eight or so months to get used to the idea, he definitely would have preferred the latter.

This whole damn situation made his head pound and his gut twist into knots. And the woman before him—innocent appearance aside—was the one responsible. If that wasn't bad enough, she honestly thought she had his whole personality— his whole life—summed up in one word: *irresponsible.*

"Look, you don't know anything about me. You knew me for less than one night. If you want to judge whether or not I have what it takes to be a father, you're going to have to stick around a lot longer than that."

"Don't worry. I plan to. But for the record, I didn't base my decision not to tell you on just one night."

"Okay, I know that's the only time we met. Unless there's something else you're not telling me."

She blanched but recovered quickly. "That's not what I meant. You don't exactly live a low-profile life. You're in the gossip columns every time you're in the country. And Messina Diamonds is in the business section when you're not."

He rocked back on his heels. "Ah, so that's what this is about."

"What?"

"Your sudden appearance on my doorstep. You were flipping through the paper one day, happened across a mention of me and put two and two together. I'm only surprised it took you this long to figure out what I was worth."

"You think this is about money?"

"What else would it be about it?"

"Not that. I can tell you that much. Financially, I'm doing just fine."

He looked around the generic two-bedroom condo. "Yeah, you're really rolling in it."

Indignation shot through her, stiffening her spine. She must have grown a full inch. "I'll have you know I make very good money. For a normal person. If I appear to live modestly, it's because I put plenty of money into my retirement fund and because I live within my means. But I do live very comfortably, thank you very much."

Her indignation was so complete he might have been convinced. If his gut wasn't screaming at him that she was hiding something.

"If it's not money you want, then what is it?"

"I just want Isabella. That's all. Is that so hard to believe?"

"Yes it is. Considering that less than twenty-four hours ago you abandoned her."

Four

"I assume this room will be sufficient."

Lucy looked around the elegantly appointed guest room. A room large enough that even the king-sized mahogany bed didn't seem out of place. The classical lines of the furniture blended beautifully with the beige raw silk duvet cover and the ecru mohair throw draped artfully across the corner of the bed. The attached guest bath, outfitted with travertine tile and buff marble, was as large as her bedroom and twice as luxurious. It was all very…cream.

The room was lovely in a blandly elegant kind of way. The rest of the house—that she'd seen so far—was the same: ridiculously spacious and decorated with refined sophistication. In short, the house looked unlived in. It wasn't a home, it was a museum. And clearly one in which a baby had never spit up her iron-fortified formula. Isabella was sure to change that.

From the corner of her eye, she shot Dex a dirty look. "Yeah. It'll do."

It would constantly remind her that she didn't belong here. That despite her protestations that she lived comfortably, the Messina definition of *comfortable* varied greatly from hers.

A reminder she didn't need and appreciated even less.

"Shall I set up this...thing?"

He held the twenty-five-pound portacrib in one hand as if it weighed no more than a briefcase.

"No. I'll do it. They can be tricky."

In truth, it wasn't that difficult. But she didn't want him feeling comfortable with any of Isabella's things. Besides, after the visit to her condo, she needed a break from him.

He looked from her to the ExerSaucer, where Isabella sat gurgling happily while she spun one of the chair's many doodads. Lucy took little comfort in how nervous he looked. But, she supposed, a little comfort was better than none.

"Well, then. I'll let you get settled. Dinner will be served at seven."

"Dinner will be served?"

"While you were packing, I called Mavis, our house-keeper, and arranged for her to make a full meal. Normally, she just leaves something in the fridge for Derek or me to heat up. But with Isabella here I figured she'd need something more."

She stared at him in confusion for a moment, trying to make sense of his words. "Isabella is five months old. She doesn't even eat baby food yet."

"Oh."

"You didn't try to feed her real food when you were alone with her, did you?"

"No. There were two cans of formula in the bag you left. I fed her those."

"Thank God."

But the way his lips tightened made her wonder if he tried the formula before or after trying to feed her a hamburger or something absurd.

"Dinner will be served at seven," he repeated. "Even if she won't eat it, presumably you will."

"Of course." He was already out the door when she muttered, "But I could have just cooked my own food like a normal human being."

He stuck his head back through the doorway. "What was that?"

"Sounds great." She smiled brightly in the face of his suspicious glare. "I'm looking forward to it."

"Yeah. That's what I thought you said." Though his expression made it clear he didn't believe anything of the sort.

This time, she followed him to the door, closed it behind him and then collapsed against it with a sigh. Across the room, Isabella sat in her ExerSaucer.

"Look at the mess your momma has gotten us into this time."

Isabella's head tilted to the side, a slightly puzzled expression on her face.

"Don't you worry, though," Lucy said, crossing to the bed where her purse lay. "I'll fix this. I promise."

Lucy dug through her purse and pulled out her cell phone. When her call was shuffled over to Jewel's voice mail, she spoke low into the phone.

"Damn it, Jewel, I need to talk to you. Still. I've got Isabella. She's fine. But I'm staying at Dex Messina's house, so don't bother trying me at home." She almost hung up, but then at the last moment added, "And by the way, I've got over a dozen books on how to take care of babies. You couldn't have stuck one of those in the diaper bag for Dex?"

As she dropped the phone back in her bag, she noticed the thin sheaf of papers she'd gotten from her lawyer just last week. Papers that would give her full custody of Isabella. Papers she hadn't yet gotten Jewel to sign.

Pulling her suitcase behind her she crossed to the dresser. She quickly unpacked her clothes into the top two drawers, carefully burying the bundle of papers beneath her stash of bras and panties.

How in the world had she found herself in this mess? And here, she'd always tried so hard to do the right thing. To be the good sister.

Sure, she'd been cleaning up her sister's messes all her life. She usually did it in her own way—logically, without lies or deception. But this? This desperate scheme to get Isabella back seemed almost like something Jewel would do. Living in Dex's house for two weeks while she pretended to be Isabella's mother? The plan was farcical. No, scratch that. It wasn't a *plan* at all. It was a series of irrational decisions held together with nothing more than hope and luck. It would never work. Except it *had* to work.

She rubbed her fingers over her forehead, wishing she could rub away the tension gathering there. Unfortunately, that was as futile as trying to coax some warmth out of Dex.

"I'm not going to let that awful man raise you."

Isabella looked toward the door and cooed. Almost as if she knew exactly which awful man Lucy was talking about. Lucy frowned. Isabella's coo hadn't sounded nearly as traumatized as Lucy would have expected, given all the poor girl had been through.

"Okay, honey, you're just going to have to take my word on this. That is not the kind of man you want raising you. He's cold and emotionally unavailable."

Not unlike her own father. After their mother had up and

walked out on them, he had left them to be raised largely by nannies and sitters. They had both suffered from his neglect in their own way.

Lucy had often thought things had been worse for Julie—this was back when she was Julie, before she'd legally changed her name to the more sophisticated Jewel.

Jewel had been their mother's darling, whereas Lucy had been largely ignored. Jewel had been spoiled and coddled, treated like a pampered lapdog. Until the day their mother had just left without warning or apology.

For Lucy, who was used to being ignored by both parents, things had gone on pretty much as they always had. Jewel, who was used to their mother's elaborate shows of affection, had pulled one outrageous stunt after another trying to get their father's attention. And when that hadn't worked, the attention of any man.

And now Jewel had done the unthinkable. She'd abandoned her own baby. But Isabella would never suffer from it. Not if Lucy had anything to say about it.

She dropped down on her knees before Isabella. "I'm not going to let that happen to you. No psychological freezer burn for you."

And Dex was certainly the kind of man to freeze out his child. She'd seen the way he'd treated Isabella so far. He hadn't held her. Had barely even looked at her.

"Here's the thing about Dex Messina. He fools a lot of people, but you can't let him fool you. He pretends to be the laid back, easygoing younger brother. The one you don't have to worry about. But you've got to keep your eye on him. Don't let him too close."

Lucy saw past that facade of his.

She'd done her research—long before she'd ever even met him. She'd read everything she could find about him.

Derek may have the reputation as the heartless business-man, but Dex wasn't to be trifled with, either. He was the brother who negotiated deals and wooed investors. The more she thought about it, the more she realized he wasn't really the black sheep of the family. No, he was the wolf in black sheep's clothing.

Definitely not the warm and responsive dad she'd choose for Isabella.

Emotionally unavailable, certainly. But cold? Maybe that wasn't quite the right word. Heat had simmered in his gaze every time he'd looked at her. His touch had nearly scalded her. Passion seemed to lurk just beneath his surface, surging forward at every reminder of the night they'd spent together.

Except *they* hadn't spent a night together.

They had never met before twenty-four hours ago.

He might remember a night of passionate sex with a tempting vixen, but it wasn't *her* he remembered. No, whatever emotion or passion he remembered was for another woman entirely.

She sighed and rocked back on her heels, resisting the urge to bury her head in her hands and just cry. Because whether or not Dex wanted her or not was completely beside the point. Because if he ever found out that she wasn't the woman he'd slept with—that she wasn't Isabella's mother—he'd guarantee she never got custody of Isabella. He'd destroy all her hopes for the future.

And she wasn't going to let that happen.

Jet lag followed by a near sleepless night up with Isabella should have been enough to knock him out com-pletely. And it did. But for only a few hours. By three in the morning he was awake again and pacing the length of the guesthouse's living room.

Not for the first time, he crossed to the bay of windows looking out over the pool. He pressed his forearm to the window and leaned his forehead to his arm. He couldn't take his eyes off the window of the room where he'd put Lucy and Isabella.

Dinner had been a chilly affair. Even little Isabella seemed to feel the tension. If he didn't know better, he'd say they'd had some kind of powwow and had mutually decided to give him the cold shoulder.

Or maybe they just both sensed how nervous he was. What did he know about babies?

Absolutely nothing.

Until last night, it had never even occurred to him that he might have one in his life.

The concept of settling down, getting married, having kids...those were just things Derek hassled him about. Which Dex had always considered ironic since Derek wasn't exactly Mr. Commitment himself.

No, Derek was one hundred percent married to his job, with only the occasional extramarital affair with things like dinner and sleep. Women ranked a distant fourth. *Marriage* might as well have been a word from another language. Dex's list might look different, but kids were just as far down it.

Except now he had one. And he didn't know what the hell to do with it.

All he knew was that he was damn sure going to do a better job than his own father had done.

Which was probably why, when he saw the light go on in Lucy's room, he immediately headed for his closet and pulled out a pair of jeans.

By the time he'd pulled them on, a procession of lights blazed from the second story east wing down to the kitchen. He slipped down the stairs and crossed the slate patio to the French doors of the kitchen, where he let himself in with his key.

Lucy looked up when he entered. She was dressed in a white cotton tank top and a pair of denim shorts that left the length of her legs exposed. Her legs were lightly tanned without being the baked brown of a woman who frequented the tanning salon. Her feet were bare, her toes painted a delicate pink.

The picture she presented would have been nearly irresistible if it hadn't been for the crying infant she held in her arms.

"She did that last night when I was taking care of her, too," he said as he typed in the code to disarm the alarm.

"Did what?"

"That crying thing. I couldn't get her to stop."

"Did you feed her?"

"No. Raina—Derek's assistant—said to give her a bottle when she woke up at one. But this was at four or five."

The look Lucy shot him said it all.

She crossed to a cabinet and pulled out a bowl, which she filled with water and then stuck in the microwave to heat. The hum from the microwave must have soothed Isabella because her crying slowed to the occasional whimper.

Lucy's silence confirmed it. She thought he was an idiot.

"Hey," he said in his defense. "She couldn't have been hungry, she'd just eaten a couple of hours earlier."

This time he could have sworn even Isabella shot him a dirty look before nuzzling her face into Lucy's neck. The scene they made, snuggling together in the dimly lit kitchen was charmingly intimate. Not to mention exclusionary.

They were a pair, those two. A family complete without him.

Resentment rushed through him. That was *his* daughter.

His daughter who cringed away from him. His daughter who cried when he held her. Whom he didn't know how to care for or feed.

All because Lucy had kept her from him. Because she'd denied him his rights.

Part of him wanted to lash out at her. Yet something held him back. Maybe it was the darkened intimacy of the kitchen. The late-night feeding. The simple domesticity of it.

He didn't want to be angry with her. He just wanted to be a part of it. To have his daughter not flinch from his touch.

The microwave beeped just as Lucy returned from the pantry with a canister of formula. She blinked as if surprised he was still there.

"You don't have to stay. I don't need your help."

"Obviously." Derek accused him of always taking the easy way out. Well, not this time. "But I'm up. And I have to learn how to do it sometime. It might as well be now."

She eyed him suspiciously for a moment, then stepped away from the can of formula. "Okay. First you wash your hands."

She guided him step by step. She stood stiffly beside him, with Isabella turned carefully away from him, almost as if Lucy didn't want her to see him preparing the bottle.

A few minutes later the bottle was warmed and he held out his arm for Isabella. Lucy frowned but handed her over. Her expression made him feel like he was ripping the infant from her arms. Isabella's instant cries of protest didn't help matters.

He lowered himself to one of the bar stools along the counter and mimicked the posture he'd seen Lucy use when she'd fed Isabella after dinner. He held Isabella out in front of him, cradled along one arm, her head in his hand, so she faced him. Her face scrunched up in apparent agony as she waved her little fists around, howling all the while.

Lucy hovered nervously behind him, ratcheting up his tension level.

"Do you want me to take her?"

"No, I can do it."

"Oh, I'm sure you can do it. But maybe you could try some other time. When she's not hungry."

He'd done some pretty crazy stuff, back before he'd settled into his current respectable position in the company. He'd crossed the Alaskan tundra in a dog sled. He'd spent a season living with a Bedouin tribe in the Sahara. He'd climbed Mount Kilimanjaro, for Christ's sake. He could do this.

He could feed one tiny infant.

Lucy must have sensed his determination because she leaned over his shoulder and wrapped her hand around his hand holding the bottle.

"You don't just shove it in her face. You have to let her know it's here if she wants it. Just rub it across her lips like this."

She moved his hands to run the bottle's nipple along Isabella's bottom lip. Slowly, Isabella's cries faded and she sucked the bottle into her mouth. She continued to gaze at him with rebellion in her eyes, but she drank greedily. Triumph surged through him.

After a moment, he became aware of Lucy's hand on his shoulder, of the warmth of her pressed against his back and along his arm. The smell of her seemed to envelope him. Something feminine and sleepy and sweet. If he turned his face, his lips would brush her cheek.

For an instant, he felt like he was part of the family. Part of the bond they shared.

Instantly, panic blossomed in his chest. *Run!* it screamed. *Get out now. Write the woman a generous check and show her the door!*

But he shoved the feeling aside, forced his heartbeat to slow and bellied up to the bar of responsibility. He wasn't that guy anymore—that guy who dodged his obligations in favor of a good time. He didn't want to be that guy. Okay, he *mostly* didn't want to be that guy.

With no appreciation for his internal struggle at all, Lucy jerked her hand away. She quickly put space between them, rounding to the other side of the counter where she bustled around the kitchen putting up the formula and rinsing out the bowl she'd heated the water in.

Isabella's eyes had drifted closed. She had one hand on the bottle, as if she was trying to hold it herself. With the other hand, she reached up and grabbed one of his fingers where it held the bottle. The tiny palm was warm against his skin. Something clenched deep within his chest.

"You do this every night?"

"Feed Isabella? Sure. It's usually only once or twice."

And she'd been doing this every night since Isabella was born. "You must be exhausted."

"Oh, it's not so bad. This time, in the middle of the night, it's kind of our time. I don't get to see her during the day when I'm at work."

"You work?" He asked the question without thinking and immediately wished he could take it back.

She stiffened, her head jerking up. "Of course I work. How did you think I supported myself?"

"What was I supposed to think? You said you could take care of Isabella during the day for the next couple of weeks."

She stilled, ducking her head. "I have to take time off work. It's not a big deal. I've got some vacation coming."

He didn't press her on this vacation time she'd be taking. It was obviously not something she wanted to talk about.

Besides which, after a few more minutes, Isabella began

to drift off to sleep, her body growing more and more relaxed, her eyes drifting closed, her rhythmic sucking slowing to just the occasional twitch.

When her mouth fell open and he pulled the bottle from her lips, his sense of accomplishment was astonishing. Mount Kilimanjaro? Bah. That was nothing.

Lucy took the bottle from him and brought it the sink to rinse out. When she returned, she held out her arms to take Isabella.

How crazy was it that he didn't want to let her go? Twenty-four hours ago, before he'd known she was his, when she was crying her head off, he would have been happy to hand her off to the first stranger who walked through the door.

But now? Now that he'd fed her and felt her fall asleep in his arms. Now that he seemed on the verge of…

Of what? He didn't know, but he just didn't want to let her go.

"I'll take her now."

He looked up at Lucy and felt the familiar stab of resentment. He had to force himself to hand Isabella back to Lucy, but he did it. After all, he wasn't the expert here, she was.

What did he really know about taking care of a baby other than it was a hell of lot harder than the sitcoms made it look.

The tender way Lucy took Isabella from his arms, the way she shushed her when she stirred and rocked gently from side to side, the almost greedy way she clutched her to her chest as she silently walked from the room—it left him wondering.

Lucy clearly adored Isabella. She would do anything for her. Hell, she'd taken two weeks of vacation so she could move into a stranger's house and care for her.

So how had this woman abandoned her baby on that same stranger's doorstep?

Once again, his gut was telling him something wasn't right with Lucy. It was time to find out what.

Five

The following afternoon, Lucy sat in her idling car, her frustrations mounting. She and Isabella had escaped the oppressive atmosphere of the house for the morning. If she had hopes of sneaking back in unnoticed, they were dashed before she even made it inside. Dex's SUV was hogging the driveway. Big, arrogant, presumptuous.

She'd never liked SUVs. They took up too much of the road. They were pushy. Insensitive to the needs of others. And this one practically gloated that it would be a better mode of transportation for Isabella.

Stifling the sudden urge to gun her car and ram the thing, she shifted into Park and set the brake.

Okay. So she was irrationally transferring her resentment to an innocent SUV. The truth was, she was scared.

Not just a little nervous, but honest to God, quaking-in-her-boots terrified that she was going to lose Isabella and that nothing short of absconding to Mexico could prevent it.

She'd been to visit her lawyer that morning. The news wasn't good. In addition to giving her a talking down the likes of which she hadn't had since grade school, he'd told her what she already knew. By bringing Dex into the equation, Jewel had really mucked up Lucy's chances of getting full custody of Isabella. Lying to him about her identity had only made things worse. Much worse.

Her lawyer had thrown around terms like "fraud" and "culpability." He was almost as bad as her own conscience.

"Damn it, damn it, damn it." She banged her head against the steering wheel with each "damn it." Unfortunately, it didn't make her feel any better. And it didn't stop her mind from racing.

So far, lying to Dex had only pushed her further away from what she wanted. When she'd decided to pretend to be Isabella's mother, it had seemed so simple.

But now she was caught in her lies. If she told him the truth, he'd never let her see Isabella again. But could she really continue to lie to him? She didn't have a choice.

A sharp rap sounded on the door frame. She jumped guiltily and whipped to face the noise.

Dex. Of course.

She pressed a palm to her chest to calm her thundering heart, then leveraged the door open and climbed out.

He eyed her suspiciously. "What's wrong?"

She couldn't meet his gaze. "You startled me. That's all." She glanced down at her watch. "It's only four. What are you even doing home?"

"I came home early to check on you. I got worried when you didn't answer the phone."

He was standing entirely too close, with one hand pressed to the roof of the car. His mere presence made her feel all jittery.

It's only because he has so much power over you.

But no matter how many times she told herself that, she wasn't sure she believed it.

"Let me guess," she quipped as she ducked under his arm to reach Isabella's door. She swung open the door so she'd at least have that barrier between them. "You thought that in an act of rebellion, Isabella had knocked me unconscious and gone out for a joy ride."

"No. I thought you'd panicked again, taken Isabella and left."

There seemed to be a note of genuine concern in his voice. She paused and looked up at him. The sun was in his eyes and he squinted as he looked down at her, making his expression unreadable.

"I would never do that."

And yet, just a few minutes ago, she'd been contemplating just that. Not seriously, true. But the thought had crossed her mind.

"I mean it," she said, and found to her surprise, she really did. "I won't just leave. I promise. I'll do everything in my power to convince you to let me keep Isabella. But I won't skip out on you."

Was it her imagination, or did he relax a little at her words?

Guilt stabbed at her conscience. Was she judging Dex unfairly? Was she assuming he was a coldhearted monster merely because that was how she wanted to see him? The thought disturbed her more than she wanted to admit.

To keep him from asking where she'd been, she lied preemptively. "I just had to stop by the office to pick up a couple of files." She held up her briefcase as evidence, thankful she'd tossed it in the back of her car last Friday before any of this had happened. "I can usually get a little work done while Isabella is sleeping."

When she stood up holding the clunky car seat, he took it from her. Together—he carrying the baby, she carrying her briefcase and the diaper bag—they walked up the driveway to the house. For a moment, they felt eerily like any normal couple meeting in the driveway after work.

"What exactly is it you do?"

"I'm an actuary."

"An actuary?"

"I crunch numbers for an insurance company. Calculate risks, that kind of thing."

"I know what an actuary does, I'm just surprised. I've never met an actuary before. I didn't expect something so—"

"Geeky," she supplied.

"That's not what I was going to say."

"No, but you were searching for a more diplomatic word for it, weren't you?"

They'd reached the door, and as he opened it, he turned to face her fully, blocking her way in with his body. "Actually I was thinking I expected something more feminine."

The appreciative gleam in his eyes sent heat spiraling through her body. Once again she was aware of how tall he was. How much bigger than her. There was something predatory in his gaze that simultaneously made her want to surrender and flee. Or just tilt her head up to his, let her eyes drift closed and wait to be kissed.

Instead, she scoffed. "Trust me. Being an actuary is the perfect job for me."

It may be geeky—which was how Jewel always described it—but it was challenging and logical. It was a no-nonsense, fuss-free kind of job. Perfect for her.

Of course, she couldn't explain any of that to Dex because he didn't know what kind of person she really was. He thought of her as the exotic, charismatic woman he'd met in a bar one night. The kind of woman who enticed men and let them pick her up for one-night stands.

No wonder he thought the job wasn't feminine enough for her.

Just one more reminder of the deception she was perpetrating. If he found out who she really was, he wouldn't be looking at her with something akin to desire in his eyes. And of course her train of thought was ridiculous, anyway. If he knew the truth, whether or not he wanted her would be the least of her concerns. Whether or not he was going to kill her with his bare hands would be a tad bit higher on the list.

Equally unsettling was the easy way they'd been talking just now. At what point had they developed this easy rapport? She didn't remember it happening. Hadn't planned on being friendly with him.

He's the monster, remember? she told herself. *He's the man who's going to take Isabella away from you. He's not friendly. He's not charming. He's ruining your life.*

He walked ahead of her, still carrying Isabella, asleep in her car seat. Lucy stood by the back door, watching him as he headed into the living room. As he settled Isabella's car seat into a darkened spot, he reached down and brushed a fingertip across her cheek.

The tender gesture made Lucy's throat close and her heart tighten. She sank against the kitchen door as her strength of will drained out of her.

He might not be a monster, but he *was* going to take Isabella away from her. Watching him in this unguarded moment brought that home in a way nothing else yet had.

Until now, despite everything, she'd had hopes that... that what? Dex would just hand Isabella over to her?

No. That wasn't going to happen. As long as he believed he was her father, he would fight for custody.

But what if...

Lucy straightened and stared blankly ahead in shock.

"What if she's not his?" Almost without meaning to, she muttered the words under her breath.

"What do you mean she might not be mine?"

She jerked her head around to find him standing not four feet away. For a long moment, Lucy simply gaped at him, panic clutching her heart.

"Well," she began nervously. "It's not like we've done a paternity test yet, right? Until then, we won't really know for sure, now will we?"

"Is there someone else who could be the father?"

Ah, there's the rub.

She didn't think so. She had been at the bar the night Jewel had hooked up with Dex. She'd watched the whole thing from a distance, shocked her sister would even flirt with one of the men who ran the company where she worked. Only later had Lucy learned that Jewel had been fired from Messina Diamonds mere days before.

As far as Lucy knew, Dex was the only man Jewel had slept with that month. And Jewel had always been one to kiss and tell. Usually in way more detail than Lucy wanted. But what if Lucy was wrong? What if she didn't know her sister as well as she thought she did?

"I don't know," she answered honestly.

He eyed her for a long, slow minute, his gaze raking across her face, no doubt looking for signs of deceit. She prayed he wouldn't find them.

Finally, he said, "It's a simple question. The month you

got pregnant, how many men did you sleep with? Just me? Or did you sleep with some other guy, too, but you left Isabella on my doorstep because I was worth more?"

For an instant, the question actually confused her. *She* hadn't slept with any men the month Isabella was conceived. But of course that wasn't what he was really asking.

And as insulting as his insinuations were, she had no one to blame but herself. After all, it was her big mouth that had gotten her into this conversation.

As annoyed with herself as she was with him, she snapped, "What makes you think it's between just you and one other guy? Maybe there were dozens."

There. That ought to shut him up.

Instead of looking shocked or even offended, he laughed. Out loud, dang it.

"Nice try." He studied her for a minute more while his laughter subsided. Shaking his head ruefully, he said, "No, I don't buy it. I don't believe for a minute there was even one other guy, let alone dozens."

"There could be," she insisted defiantly.

"No. There couldn't be. You just aren't the type. You know what I think? I think our one night together was out of character for you."

He stepped closer to her, and she found herself backing up against the door.

"You don't know me well enough to know anything about my character," she protested. She was surprised how breathless her voice sounded, how weak her protest was. How the pounding of her own heart seemed to close in on her.

"Ah," he murmured, reaching up to tuck a lock of her hair behind an ear. "But I'm an excellent judge of character. And you don't strike me as the kind of woman who's been with a lot of men. You're too innocent for that."

She felt a blush moving into her cheeks and cursed herself. Jewel wouldn't blush at this. Jewel never blushed.

"Look at you," he continued, brushing the backs of his knuckles against her hot cheeks. "You're blushing. Women who've slept with a dozen men in a month don't blush."

Trying for far more bravado than she felt, she knocked his hand away and said, "Oh, and I suppose you know women like that."

But he chuckled and ignored her. "Besides you're an actuary."

"So?"

"Actuaries don't take risks. They think things through. They plan. They organize."

She couldn't deny it. And why would she want to. She'd always taken such pride in her logical approach to life.

Yet standing here, with Dex so close she could feel the heat of his body… So close she could smell him, musky and masculine. And dangerous. She wanted to be the kind of woman who did take risks. Who threw caution to the wind.

"No," he continued, stroking her jawline with a light, tremor-inducing touch. "I bet our night together was a once-in-a-lifetime thing. I bet it really threw you for a loop. I bet you've been wondering how you could ever have done such a thing."

Of course, he was right. How many times had she wondered just that? How could Jewel sleep with men she barely knew? How could she engage in such reckless, selfish behavior?

And yet, in that instant, Lucy knew exactly how Jewel must feel. She wanted a little recklessness herself. She craved that wild restless heat.

"And I bet you haven't stopped thinking about it for a

minute. I bet you're even wondering what it would be like if it happened again."

She was. Which was why, when he leaned down to kiss her, she rose on her toes meet him.

Six

Kissing Lucy was pure heaven.

Her lips were soft and silky. Her mouth, warm and sensual. The heat of response shocked him. She didn't just kiss him back, she plastered herself against him, pouring herself into the kiss.

Her lips parted almost instantly, her body pressing up to his, her tongue stroking against his with an eagerness that inflamed his blood.

Even as he felt his body hardening in response, he knew he'd been right about her innocence. There was no expertise in her. No pretense or artifice.

Just passion.

And he couldn't wait to explore that passion.

His hands sought her hips, pulling her even closer, his fingers slipping up under her shirt to the silky skin of her midriff.

A moment later, he filled his palm with her breast. She moaned low in her throat as he rubbed his thumb across her nipple.

He couldn't get enough of her.

He wanted more. More than this teenage groping. He wanted her naked and arching against him.

But before he could maneuver her toward a horizontal surface, she pressed her palms against his chest and shoved.

He pulled back from her, satisfied that at least she was breathing even harder than he was.

"That was a mistake," she said almost immediately.

"I disagree." He'd stopped kissing her, but he wasn't about to stop touching her altogether. His hand lingered at her hip, relishing her voluptuousness, the lush generosity of her body. "In fact, I can't imagine why we haven't done this before."

"Stop that," she ordered, swatting at his hand and moving out of his reach. "We haven't done this before because it's a bad idea. We can't get involved."

He raised his eyebrows. "We have a child together. We're already involved."

She glared at him, her eyebrows knitting into a fierce frown. "I meant, involved beyond that."

Damn, but she was cute when she was trying to look fierce.

"I know what you meant. But we've already slept together once. There's nothing keeping us from doing it again."

"That's male logic for you," she quipped.

"No, that's just logic. But if that doesn't work, how about this. We're adults. We want each other, that should be enough."

"But it isn't. Regardless of whether we want—" she stumbled over the word *want* and another blush crept into her cheeks "—each other, there are other things to consider.

You said it yourself, we're adults. To me at least, that means we act responsibly. We don't just do whatever we want the instant we want to do it."

The way she emphasized the word *responsibly* set his teeth on edge. "Don't you think it's a little late to be lecturing me about responsible behavior?"

She seemed to be biting back a response. Or maybe just searching for an answer that would turn the conversation to her liking.

"Whatever else I may have done in the past, you've got to believe that now my biggest concern is doing what's right for Isabella." Her voice was hot with emotion, dense with yearning to make him understand. "I know I've made mistakes, but from here on out, I swear I'm always going to put her first. And she deserves more than two parents who would make a bad situation worse because of a momentary flash of desire."

With that, she scooped Isabella's car seat off the floor and escaped toward her room with the still-sleeping child.

He let her go, smart enough to realize she was right about one thing. This wasn't the time.

For one thing, he still had too many questions about her. If he was right—and he'd bet half his fortune he was—and she really was that inexperienced, then what had she been doing in that bar fourteen months ago?

Why after years of cautious, responsible behavior had she picked him for her one-night stand?

If they'd met under other circumstances, he might have believed her uncharacteristic behavior that night was due entirely to the chemistry between them.

But she had approached him. And when she'd done so, she hadn't been timid or shy. She'd been bold and flirtatious in a way he hadn't seen since. She'd set out to seduce him. Which again brought him back to the question: why *him?*

Only one answer came to mind. She must have known about his money.

And if she'd known about his money, he wondered if she'd gotten pregnant on purpose. Had this seemingly sweet and innocent woman targeted him for a pregnancy scam for money?

Every bone in his body said she wasn't capable of doing that. Yet he knew she was lying about something.

Just that afternoon, he'd visited Quinton McCain. Quinn ran McCain Security, the firm that handled all the security for Messina Diamonds. He also happened to be one of Dex's best friends.

As head of his own very successful company, digging up dirt wasn't exactly the kind of thing Quinn normally did, but when Dex had explained the situation, Quinn hadn't blinked an eye. He'd merely whipped out his BlackBerry, jotted down what little Dex knew about Lucy and promised to find whatever dirt there was. Dex had the nagging suspicion Quinn wouldn't find much.

If conning money out of Dex had been her plan all along, why had Lucy waited so long to execute it? Why not come to him when she was pregnant? Why struggle through raising an infant alone for five months? And why had she left Isabella on his doorstep at all?.

He kept coming back to that question. He simply couldn't reconcile the woman he knew with that one action. The longer he knew her, the more absurd it seemed that she'd done it at all.

Shaking his head, he crossed to the fridge, pulled out a cold Shiner and twisted off the cap. He sipped it as he crossed the patio to the guesthouse.

He needed something to clear his head, so he changed into his swim trunks and headed for the pool to swim laps.

As he stood poised on the diving board, he couldn't help wondering if Lucy was right. Maybe Isabella did deserve more.

But she was wrong about at least one thing. This wasn't some fleeting flash of desire. She may not have enough experience to know better, but he did. The chemistry between them was off the charts. Merely avoiding each other for the next two weeks wouldn't make it go away. At some point, they were going to have to deal with it.

Laps in a cold pool wouldn't work forever.

From the window of her room, Lucy watched Dex dive into the pool. As his lean, muscled body cut effortlessly through the water, she tried to tell herself she'd made the right choice. She'd made the *only* choice.

Her first concern had to be Isabella's welfare. Her own wants and needs were irrelevant.

Oh, but she had *wanted*. His kiss had sparked a fire in her she hadn't imagined she could feel. His touch had made her tremble. Even now, her breasts felt overly sensitive. Her blood seemed to pound, throbbing between her legs.

Frustrated, she spun away from the window and crossed to sit in the armchair beside Isabella's car seat. She crossed her legs, pressed them together, but that did little to ease the ache.

Damn him.

Damn him for making her want what she couldn't have. For making her miss what she'd resisted for so long.

He was right of course. It had been years—forever, it seemed—since she'd been with a man. So many of her previous relationships had been mediocre at best. And she wasn't Jewel, jumping carelessly from one man to the next, mindless of the risks such behavior incurred. She could never be so cavalier with her body or her emotions.

And now, apparently, she was paying the price in sexual frustration. Maybe if she had a fling every couple of months, she wouldn't now be in the position of desiring the one man she shouldn't want.

Lucy was avoiding him.

He'd come home earlier and earlier each night, yet every time Mavis had handed him his warmed-over food and told him Lucy had already eaten and was up in her room, "Trying to put Isabella down."

By day four, the phrase set his teeth on edge, probably because it evoked images of lame racehorses being shot out behind the stables.

Why Lucy's obvious avoidance of him bothered him so, he couldn't say. But he hadn't felt this ignored since childhood, and that sure as hell wasn't an experience he wanted to revisit.

He told himself he should just be glad she was making this fatherhood thing so easy on him. So far, other than that first day he'd had Isabella all by himself, he'd done almost nothing to take care of her. He should be rejoicing. Instead, he was just plain irritated.

Which was why he left work at two on Friday, to force his way through the already chocked downtown traffic, to make it home by three in the afternoon. Unless Lucy was going to have Mavis smuggle her food up to her room, then damn it, she was going to eat her meal with him.

He bypassed the guesthouse altogether and headed straight for the main house, determined to catch Lucy in person. He stopped a few feet into the living room to stare at the scene before him.

The living room furniture had been shoved aside. Lucy had covered the floor with several fluffy cream-colored blankets, all of which bore suspicious brown splotchy stains. Mavis—who before today Dex had never once seen crack a smile—sat cross-legged on the floor, jostling a giggling Isabella on her knee while dangling a chain of plastic links before her grasping hands. Lucy lay on the floor beside them, her head propped up on one of the sofa's pillows, her bare feet resting on the edge of one of his brother's priceless Eames leather chairs. Mozart's "Eine Kleine Nachtmusik" played softly in the background. Over the music, Lucy was reading aloud from a paperback, the cover of which she'd folded back, so that she held it in one hand.

"'This little explanation with Mr. Knightly gave Emma considerable pleasure.'" A bowl of red grapes sat by her other hand, and she paused to pop a handful in her mouth before continuing. "'It was one of the agreeable recollections of the ball.'"

At that moment, Mavis looked up. For a second, she stared at him incomprehensibly, as if she didn't recognize him or couldn't imagine why he'd shown up to disrupt their idyllic afternoon.

"Miss Lucy." Mavis cleared her throat and sent a pointed look in his direction.

"'She was extremely glad…'" Lucy trailed off as she turned her head to glance in his direction. "Oh." She swung her feet off the chair and sprang up from her reclined position, knocking over the bowl of grapes in the progress. "Oh. Dex. What are you doing here?"

"I live here."

"But it's a Friday." She didn't meet his gaze, but hustled to pluck up the grapes, which were rolling haphazardly around the hills and wrinkles of the blanket. "In the middle of the afternoon. Shouldn't you be at work?"

"One of the benefits of being a VP," he said tersely.

Why did it bother him, how relaxed and calm she'd been just a moment ago and how nervous and tense she now seemed?

"Oh." She dropped a few more of the meandering grapes back into the bowl. "Yes. I suppose."

She stood and as she did so, he heard a faint pop and at the same time an expression of surprise crossed her face. "Oh." This time she muttered it with a cringe. She lifted her foot to reveal a squashed grape on the ball of her foot and a bright, oblong stain on the blanket. She sighed. "Well, I suppose we wouldn't have been able to get the formula stains out, anyway."

Mavis stood as well, clucking sympathetically. "Never you worry. It's just a comforter." She waved a hand dismissively. "I'll have it replaced and Mr. Derek will never know the difference."

Mavis shot him an angry glare as if daring him to whip out his cell phone and tattle on them that very instant. Then she handed Isabella over to Lucy and dusted her hands off on the dish towel she had hanging from the waistband of her khaki pants. Then she pulled the dish towel out and handed it to Lucy as well, who used it to wipe off her foot.

"Well, dinner won't be cooking itself, now will it?" she muttered as she huffed off in the direction of the kitchen, shooting him one last rebellious look.

"So." He shoved his hands into his pockets. "This is how you've been spending your days."

Lucy shifted Isabella into her other arm, without meeting his gaze. "Yes. I suppose it is." She passed the dish towel from one hand to the other as if unsure where to put it.

"Seems fun."

She bristled visibly and her eyes shot up to his. "This isn't just a vacation for me, if that's what you're implying."

"It wasn't."

"I rarely get to spend whole days with Isabella like this, but when I do, I make the most of our time."

"I didn't—"

"Listening to music, particularly classical music, has been shown in countless studies to increase a child's cognitive math and reasoning skills. And reading aloud to children, even babies, helps them develop a love of literature."

"I'm sure she's really enjoying—" he glanced down at the paperback Lucy had discarded when he'd entered "—*Emma,* is it?"

Lucy's already stiff spine straightened even more. "You think this is just a big joke?"

"Not at all."

She stomped off the blanket and bent down to pick it up. "I'll have you know, I take this very seriously."

Mozart continued to lilt in the background, a discordant backdrop to her harsh tone.

"Obviously."

Still holding Isabella, she struggled to bunch up the king-sized comforter. "Well, I'm sure you have more important things to do than belittle my work with Isabella. So we'll just get out of your way so you can have the living room all to yourself."

With that, she spun on her heel—as much as she could—and stalked—or rather tried to—from the room, the blanket trailing behind her like a train.

"Lucy, wait." The words left his mouth before he could stop himself.

She stopped but didn't turn around.

What was he doing? Why wasn't he just letting her go?

This was exactly the kind of emotional entanglement he'd spent his whole life avoiding. He'd never wanted a kid. Certainly not with a woman like Lucy. Not with someone he couldn't trust. So why didn't he just let her walk away? Why *couldn't* he let her walk away?

He didn't know. But he did know this—he'd come home early because he wanted—no, needed—to spend time with Isabella. Not just Isabella.

"I didn't come home early to belittle you."

Slowly she turned to face him, her expression guarded, her arms overflowing with both baby and comforter.

"I haven't seen you or Isabella in four solid days. There's no point in you living here with her if I never get to see her."

Lucy narrowed her gaze in a calculated manner, then gave a slight huff of indignation. "I couldn't agree more. I'll pack up our things and be out of here within the hour."

"That's not what I meant."

A sigh deflated her chest. "I was afraid of that."

"If this—" he gestured to spot in the living room where they'd been lounging "—is what you do with her during the day, then I'd like to—" he hesitated, looking for the right word "—participate."

"How?"

He crossed to her, mincing around the comforter and taking it from her arms. "Let's start by putting this back. And you can show me what you normally do with her."

She frowned as he spread the blanket out over the floor. "It's not complicated," she hedged.

And he could see from the glint in her eyes, she was looking for an excuse to bail on him.

"But as you said, it's important. Why don't you talk me through it?"

He kicked off his shoes and settled down on the comforter with his back against the sofa.

"Well," she began hesitantly. "She can't roll over yet, but she's close."

"Okay."

"So she needs a lot of belly time." When he looked at her blankly, Lucy added, "To strengthen her neck and arm muscles." She sat down a few feet away from him. "Here, like this."

She placed Isabella on her belly on the blanket and then lay down beside her, so their faces were at eye level. Isabella automatically wedged her arms under her shoulders and levered herself up to get a better look at Lucy.

"That's great, Isabella."

Isabella grinned in delight at her success.

Once again feeling excluded, Dex lowered himself to Isabella's other side. When he was at her level, she twisted to get a look at him, flashing him one of her adorable toothless grins. A band of emotion tightened around his heart.

He gazed past Isabella to Lucy, wanting to share the moment with her. For a moment, she just stared back, her eyes wide. Then she sucked in an audible breath and jerked to a sitting position.

"Well, looks like you've got that down pat." She scrambled back toward the chair. "If you want I can just leave you two alone."

"Aren't you going to read?"

"Read?"

"Yeah. You were reading to her when I came in. Didn't you say it would improve her cognitive abilities or something?"

"Um…yes. Something like that." Lucy fumbled to pick up the worn copy of *Emma* before raising herself to the chair and tucking her feet under her self-consciously.

As she flipped through the book to the spot she'd left off at in chapter thirty-nine, she was all too aware of her heart pounding in her chest. She didn't want to consider why it was beating so fast, though it seemed all too likely that Dex was the cause. The intolerable man was as sexy as he was annoying.

And what did he mean, coming home in the middle of a workday just so he could bond with Isabella? What was he doing, trying to be a real father? Ha! Likely story.

His appearance here just reminded her that she was living on borrowed time. What she needed was a plan of action. A surefire way to convince Dex that he should hand Isabella over to her. And maybe—just maybe—she knew just what needed to be done.

Seven

"I'm sorry," she lied. "There's nothing I can do about it."

Dex's expression was grim, but he nodded. "No problem."

"Are you sure? You'll be all alone with her for four, maybe five hours."

His mouth tightened, but when he spoke he sounded more resolute than scared. "I'll handle it. If you can't get out of this business dinner, then I'll watch her while you're gone."

It had been several days since he'd kissed her. In that time he'd made no further attempts.

She, however, had been very busy. She'd spent her time hatching a plan guaranteed to make him lose confidence in himself as a father.

It was ruthless. It was cruel. But it was for Isabella's own good.

Massive twinges of guilt aside, it was a good plan. She was going to leave Isabella alone with Dex for the evening.

Sure, it seemed simple enough, but Lucy had spent enough evenings alone with Isabella to know they could be brutal. The hours from six to ten were often fraught with crying, colic, sleeplessness and general fussiness. Plus, Isabella hadn't napped well today, so tonight was likely to go particularly badly.

As if to prove Lucy's point, Isabella picked that moment to scrunch up her face and let out a wail.

Dex shot a look of grim determination toward Isabella, who had been lounging innocently in her bouncy chair on the living room floor.

"Is there a number where you can be reached?"

Lucy sighed, as if it were a huge imposition, before rattling off her cell-phone number. "But this is a very important meeting for me. Call only if it's a true emergency."

He nodded as he typed the number into his own cell phone. "Got it. Only in an emergency."

And she felt only a teeny tiny bit guilty about leaving him alone with Isabella. He wanted to be a father? Well, here was his chance. This was what being a parent was all about. Making it through the rough times. Learning how to do it on your own.

She'd had plenty of nights when Isabella hadn't stopped crying no matter what she'd tried. Plenty of nights she'd wanted to pull out her hair. Or had wanted to just shoot Jewel for blithely going about her own life while she left Lucy to care for her daughter.

The simple truth was, this parenting gig wasn't for pansies.

And if she didn't leave now, she might not have the strength to put him through this ordeal, even though it was her last chance to convince him to give her Isabella.

She grabbed her purse and headed out. She turned one last time at the door. Dex stood under the imposing arch doorway leading from the foyer to the living room. His hands were on his hips as he stared down at the tiny crying Isabella.

"You going to be okay?" But she wasn't one-hundred-percent sure if it was a question or meant to be reassurance.

He looked up at her, his gaze steely and focused. "We'll be fine."

She nodded, but as she closed the door behind her and headed for her car, she knew they wouldn't.

Dex stared at Isabella for a long minute before letting panic settle over him. What kind of diabolical scheme was Lucy up to now?

He could hardly protest when she'd asked him to watch Isabella for a couple of hours tonight. After all, she'd been caring for her nonstop for a full week. Well, who was he kidding, for the past five months. Who was he to complain about just one night?

After all, he could do this. He'd been alone with her before and nothing bad had happened. Sure, she'd cried a lot and he'd ended up with a headache, but he could do this.

He could, he repeated to himself as he bent down, unlatched the straps from the seat and picked her up.

If possible, her cries grew even louder. She swung her fists toward his face like a tiny boxer, her lovely face turning red from exertion.

He held her at eye level to scope out the situation. Assess the damage. This was just a problem like any other. He could solve it. He just needed the right approach.

But man, was it good for her to be crying like this?

Great sobs shook her body and finally she had to pause to suck in a shuddering breath, before letting out another howl of outrage.

"Okay, there are only a few things that could be wrong with you to make you cry like this."

At the sound of his voice, Isabella's crying slowed. She opened her eyes to glare at him. She snuffled as if waiting to hear his opening offer.

"You could have a dirty diaper." He shifted her in his arms to peek through the leg of the tiny pink jumper she wore. "Nope. Not it. You could be hungry."

Except he'd seen Lucy feed her a bottle just before leaving.

"You could be tired. In which case you'll fall asleep before long."

Except he knew there were plenty of times he'd been traveling all day when he was just too tired to fall asleep. Hopefully that wouldn't be the case here.

Dex rattled off the next few options quickly, feeling less and less optimistic about them.

"You could miss Lucy. You could know that you're in the hands of an amateur. You could be panicking because you know I don't know what the hell I'm doing.

"And if that's the case, then we're both screwed."

Unfortunately, he'd been right.

Two hours later, after countless diaper changes, several warmed and then tossed bottles of formula, and what he was sure were ruptured eardrums, Dex could finally imagine why Lucy had left Isabella on his doorstep. Five months of this, and he might be willing to do the same.

In the end, he'd resorted to doing what he'd seen Lucy do to soothe her. He'd held her close to his chest, hummed in her ear and waltzed around the living room. By the time she started to calm down, his own pulse was returning to normal. After a solid forty-five minutes of waltzing, he was ready for a break. Since she seemed nearly asleep, he danced toward the sofa and sank to the edge.

Her eyes immediately opened and she let out a mewling protest.

"Come on, Izzie. Don't look at me like that. You just quieted down."

Remarkably, instead of howling her outrage, she cocked her head to the side, blinked her impossibly wide blue eyes at him and seemed to listen.

As soon as he settled back on the sofa to relax, she screwed up her face again and looked ready to scream, so he kept talking.

"I had no idea babies were this much work. Sure, you see little kids wreaking havoc at restaurants and stores, but those are the older ones. By then, they're mobile. They can get into trouble. Play with matches, that kind of thing."

The truth was, the sum total of his experience with infants was what had happened in the past week. For him, Izzie was it.

"I suppose I had it coming, though. I was the trouble-maker in the family. Derek—your uncle—he was so serious, even as a kid. Never a step out of line for that guy. Me, I was the one climbing out the second-story window to jump from the roof into the big pile of leaves in the lawn."

Thank God, he'd broken only one leg with that stunt. He'd nearly given his mother a heart attack.

He chuckled as he remembered how she'd yelled at him, shaking her fists, her face all red with anger. She could sure throw a fit, his mother could, back before the cancer had sapped all her strength and left her too weak to fight back.

To Izzie he said, "Your grandmother would have loved to have seen you."

Instead, she hadn't lived to see either of her own children even make it out of high school.

And because she seemed to be listening, he told Izzie about his mom and all the things she'd missed in his life.

About how she'd died when he was only ten. How she'd married a poor, ornery geologist who'd believed there were diamonds to be mined in the Northwest Territories of Canada when everyone else thought he was crazy. How she'd died without ever losing faith in her husband, even though he wasn't proved right until years later.

"That very first diamond Dad found, he had set in a ring for her, even though she'd never wear it. He always said she was the love of his life and there'd never be anyone to replace her."

And there hadn't been. Not in the nineteen long years from her death until his.

Dex leaned back, propped his feet against the coffee table and rested Izzie against his legs, where he could look at her. During one of the many diaper changes, he'd given up the pink jumper. Now she was dressed only in her diaper, leaving her cubby little belly exposed.

With a resolute nod, he reached into his pocket and pulled out the box from the jeweler he'd visited over lunch.

Holding Izzie with one hand, he flipped up the top of the box to reveal the thin platinum chain and the simple diamond solitaire ring dangling from it.

Just before his father's death, he'd given the ring to Dex, extracting the promise that someday he'd give it to the love of *his* life. Today, Dex had had a jeweler attach the ring to a necklace for Isabella.

"You're a little young for it, Izzie, but I figure…" He hesitated, choked back a surge of emotion and finished with, "Hell, it's a family heirloom if nothing else."

He held the box out to her and she reached one tiny finger toward the ring. He pulled the chain from the box and let it dangle from his hand. The ring spun back and forth, the diamond catching in the light. Izzie reached for it, smiling with delight when he pulled it from her grasp.

Something bloomed deep inside of him as he gazed at her toothless grin.

Once again he was struck with amazement. This child was his. This perfect little human being had come from him.

He'd spent all his adult life avoiding emotional commitments. Keeping everyone at arm's length. It's the way he'd wanted it.

But now? Now that Izzie was here, he wasn't so sure anymore. Yeah, he could push her away like he had everyone else in his life, but would that be fair to her? Maybe it would be. After all, what did he know about being a father? Maybe Izzie's childhood would be happier if he just bowed out now. Quietly walked away and let Lucy raise her.

Yet every cell in his body rebelled at the idea of never seeing her again.

Besides, wasn't pawning her off on Lucy just taking the easy way out? He thought briefly of his own miserable childhood. How many times had he berated his parents for putting their own wants and needs before his. If he bailed on Izzie now, wouldn't he be doing the same?

And that's when it hit him. She wasn't crying. He wasn't stressed. They'd been alone for nearly three hours. He really *could* do this. He could be a father to Isabella.

Whatever else he needed to know, he could learn on the way.

As he swung the ring back and forth in front of Isabella, he felt a deep contentment settle over him.

His cell phone rang just as she grabbed the chain in her tiny fist. He let go of his end to reach into his pants pocket and dig the phone out.

He frowned when he spied the listing. Lucy.

"How's it going?"

"Great," he answered honestly, relieved she hadn't called an hour ago when Izzie was screaming her head off.

"Really?"

"Yes, really."

"She isn't crying."

He couldn't tell if it was a question or if she was commenting on the lack of squalling in the background.

"No. She quieted down about an hour ago. We're doing great."

And that's when he looked back at Izzie and didn't see the chain in her hand.

"That's...fantastic," Lucy said unenthusiastically.

But her comment barely registered.

"Great. See ya soon," he muttered and hung up without waiting for a reply.

Where was the necklace?

What in the world could she have done with it?

She gurgled contentedly, one tiny fist shoved entirely into her mouth. He stared at her for a long minute as dread built in his stomach.

"Oh...you didn't. Tell me you didn't put it in your mouth."

She actually giggled in response. The little imp.

After gently prying her fist out, he ran his forefinger along the inside of her mouth. Nothing.

He held Isabella up in both hands, hoping the necklace would fall to the floor. It didn't. He had to resist the urge to shake her lightly to see if it would drop out.

He dusted himself off. He dusted her off. He ran his hand

across the cushions of the sofa. He even got down on his knees and ran his hand along the floor and under the sofa.

Then he rocked back on his knees, clutched her to his chest, and fought the urge to panic.

Damn it.

How could he have made such a rookie mistake?

And why did Isabella have to pay for his stupidity?

Standing, he grabbed his cell phone from the sofa and quickly scrolled through the numbers to the home number of Derek's secretary. Thank God she'd just gotten back from Antwerp.

"Raina, this is Dex," he said when she answered after six rings.

"Dex?" There was a sleepy note in her voice that vanished almost instantly. "What's wrong? Has Derek been in an accident?"

"Derek? No. I'm here with the baby. I think she may have swallowed something. What do I do?"

"Okay." There was a beleaguered sigh from the other end of the phone. "Well, first off, she's not choking on it, is she?"

"I don't think so. How would I know?"

"Is she turning blue? Not breathing? Any of those things?"

"No. She's still breathing."

"That's good. But for the record, if she ever is choking, you don't call me, you call 9-1-1, got it?"

"Got it. And Raina, I'm sorry about this." And he truly was. Derek pulled this kind of crap with Raina all the time—using her like his personal slave, calling her in the middle of the night. "I didn't know who else to call."

Of course he could have called Lucy, but she'd been waiting for him to fail.

"No problem. Okay, as long as she's not choking, don't

panic. But you should take her to the doctor. They'll know what to do." He heard the rap-tap-tap of computer keys in the background. "There's a children's hospital just down the tollway from your house. I'll get you the address."

He squeezed his eyes shut as he paced back and forth, holding Isabella in one hand and the phone in the other.

"But, Dex, you should know. They may make this difficult for you. If she has to be admitted to the hospital, they'll need to see her birth certificate. When you can't provide it, they'll have to call CPS."

He thanked Raina, hung up and began putting Isabella in her car seat. He would have to call Lucy after all. She could meet them at the hospital. She'd have the birth certificate if it came to that. But even if they did have to call CPS, that was okay, too. Nothing mattered but making sure Isabella was safe.

Eight

The doctor was one of those gratingly jovial types destined to drive parents crazy in a time of crisis. However, the nurse more than made up for his attitude with her disapproving, scornful frowns.

"Well, well, well." The doctor flashed them a broad grin and chucked Isabella under the chin. "Swallowed a necklace, did you?"

The nurse looked at her clipboard, then glared at Lucy. "And a diamond ring, according to the chart. Who was watching the child when this happened?"

Lucy sensed Dex about to answer, but she didn't let him. "What does it matter? Accidents like this happen." She turned her attention to the doctor. "What can you do?"

"Well, first, we'll have to take an X-ray. See how far down the intestinal tract the necklace has made it. Of course, our main concern will be the chain catching in her stomach or intestines. If the X-ray shows the necklace hasn't progressed very far, we may just fish it out."

Beside her, Dex paled, but nodded resolutely. Lucy squeezed his hand.

The doctor took Isabella from Dex's arms. "Little lady, you sure are making your parents worry tonight." The doctor wrinkled his nose. "And unless I'm mistaken, the first procedure you're going to need is a diaper change."

If possible, the nurse's expression soured even more, as if this was the final insult. The ultimate proof they were unworthy parents.

Lucy felt her cheeks heat. In the anxiety of the moment, she hadn't even thought to check Isabella's diaper. She took the baby from the doctor. "I'll do that."

"I didn't bring the diaper bag." Dex's expression was crestfallen. Apparently, he wasn't invulnerable to the nurse's disapproval, either.

She laid her hand on his arm. "Don't worry. I carry a spare diaper and some wipes in my purse."

The doctor and nurse left them alone in the exam room so they could change the diaper. As she went through the familiar motions, her mind raced.

Logically, she knew kids swallowed things all the time. Usually, they just passed right through. But that didn't keep her from worrying.

What if she needed surgery? Oh, God. An anesthetic. She was so young for surgery. What if…

Then she looked down. Actually looked at what she was doing.

"Dex, you thought she swallowed a ring, right?"

"Yes."

"A solitaire. Not too big. Half carat maybe?"

"Yeah."

Lucy chuckled as relief flooded over her. She stepped back so Dex could look at the open diaper. There, right on top, was the ring. Dirty and definitely in need of cleaning, but intact.

"She didn't swallow it, Dex. She stuck it down her diaper."

It was the obvious conclusion since there was no way it could have passed so quickly.

Dex scowled as he stared at the incontrovertible evidence before him. "She had to have swallowed it. I looked everywhere."

"I guess—" Giggles welled up inside of her and she paused, sagging against the exam table, feeling weak and giddy. "I guess you didn't think to look there."

Dex seemed more irritated than relieved. Somehow his annoyance only made her giggle more.

He didn't see the humor in the situation. "Why would she do that?"

"She's a baby. They stick things down their diapers. It happens." Suppressing the last of her giggles, she continued. "Besides, in her defense, that diaper was on very loose."

This earned her a glare. "You finish changing the diaper. I'll go tell the doctor."

Dex all but stomped from the room, his frustration palpable.

Which somehow just made the whole situation funnier to Lucy.

She chuckled as she used a wipe to fish out the ring. A few more wipes and Isabella was clean and tucked into a fresh diaper.

For a long moment, she stared at the ring dangling on its delicate platinum chain. When he'd mentioned losing a ring, she'd wondered—absently and beneath her fear— what he'd been doing carrying around a diamond solitaire. After all, diamond rings were the classic engagement ring.

The thought had flashed through her mind—however briefly—that he might be thinking of asking her to marry him. After all, that would be the ultimate easy way out. Why hire a nanny when you can marry one instead?

Thank goodness he hadn't done that. She saw now that had never been his intention. The ring had been attached to the necklace by a single link of chain, and the necklace itself was exactly the length for a girl. This wasn't a ring meant to be worn by an adult, but around a child's neck.

Funny how relieved she was that he hadn't planned the blundering mistake of asking her to marry him purely for his own convenience. She didn't think she could have borne it if he had.

After folding the rather dirty ring into the baby wipe, she tucked it carefully into the inner pocket of her purse and returned her attention to Isabella.

"Don't you worry about Mr. Grumpy there," she cooed as she leaned over Isabella to fasten on the new diaper. Lucy couldn't resist blowing a raspberry on the sweet, chubby belly. Isabella giggled in delight. "You just gave him a scare, you little bugger. That's the only reason he's so grumpy."

Slowly, Lucy straightened. Staring straight ahead, she mused aloud, "You really did give him a scare."

Dex had been terrified. Really, truly freaked out.

In fact, he'd been more upset than she had. Now, true, he didn't have as much experience with kids. He hadn't yet lived through the dozens of little traumas babies put their parents through. The scares and anxieties.

Not that she was actually Isabella's mother. She was just the aunt. Nevertheless, she felt all of the worries as deeply as any mother could.

She just hadn't expected him to feel them, too.

Earlier that day, if someone had asked her how Dex would respond in this situation, she never would have imagined his palpable fear and genuine distress.

Mindlessly, she put the wipes back into her purse. She picked up Isabella before crossing to the sink and washing her hands. But her mind was racing.

She'd been so sure that Dex wouldn't be a good father. So sure, he was cold and unemotional. Exactly the kind of father she didn't want for Isabella.

Everything she'd done had been predicated on that assumption. All the lies she'd told. All the deception. All because she'd been so sure—so sure!—Dex didn't really care about Isabella.

But what if she'd been wrong?

Dex drove back to the house alone, having put Isabella and her car seat back into Lucy's car and into Lucy's care. Where she belonged.

His hands clenched the steering wheel with a grip almost as firm as the one tension had over his body. Recrimination after recrimination pounded through his head.

Of all the stupid mistakes. What kind of an idiot gives a baby a ring to play with? What kind of an idiot doesn't think to check the diaper once he'd lost it?

If he had checked Isabella's diaper, then at least he wouldn't have had to call Lucy. At least she wouldn't have known about his stupidity. But he probably would have told her anyway. No, she needed to know about his incompetence.

Of course, his mistake, minor as it was, was nothing in comparison to the many, much bigger mistakes he'd made tonight. The truth was, they were lucky. They'd gotten off easy. No help from him.

It all came down to this. He didn't know jack about being a father. And knew even less about caring for an infant.

He pulled into the driveway to find Lucy had arrived before he had. She was bent over, removing an already sleeping Isabella from her car seat.

Izzie opened her eyes blearily, then fisted a hand around Lucy's shirt, nuzzled her neck and drifted peacefully back to sleep. A few minutes later, when Lucy laid her down in the crib that had been set up in her room, Izzie didn't even stir.

Watching Lucy bend over Izzie's crib, he felt his chest compress with relief and mingled fear. Tonight, he'd come so close to losing her. To losing them both.

He sure as hell didn't blame Lucy for the distant, cold look in her eyes when she straightened and found him standing in the doorway.

As she shut her bedroom door behind her, she whispered, "I suppose we need to talk about this." She shoved her hands into her back pockets as she headed down the stairs. "And you're certainly not the type to put things off, are you?"

"And here I thought you'd be eager to rake me over the coals. After all, you've been proven right."

She didn't answer until they'd reached the living room and he got the impression that she'd been searching for the right words.

"Yes. I suppose you would think that." She sank down to the sofa, propped her elbows on her knees and looked up at him, regret lining her every feature. "I expected you to fail tonight. I was *counting* on it."

"And I never doubted I wouldn't," he admitted, not bothering to hide his chagrin. Since his fear was still palpable, he crossed to the bar, poured himself a brandy. After glancing at her, he poured a second. If her nerves were half as rattled as his, she needed it. "I'm not used to failure."

She took a tiny sip of her brandy and swallowed her grimace. "No. I don't suppose you are. But what happened tonight wasn't your failure. It wasn't your mistake. It was mine."

"Lucy—"

"No, let me finish." She stood, setting the brandy snifter on the coffee table. "I didn't have a business meeting. That was just an excuse to leave you alone with Isabella." Guilt echoed in her voice. "I knew you couldn't handle it. I knew you weren't prepared. This is all my fault."

She sounded so dejected, he wanted to pull her into his arms. Instead, he smiled ruefully. "You wanted me to see how difficult it was. You thought I'd realize how hard it was and I'd give up. That I'd let you take Isabella."

She looked at him in surprise. "You knew what I was up to?"

"You didn't really think you could out-strategize me, did you?"

"Yes, I suppose I did." She laughed ruefully. "And here I thought I was being so clever."

"Don't be so hard on yourself. You were right. I don't have what it takes."

Once again, surprise flickered across her face. "But you do."

Now it was his turn to laugh bitterly. "Right. I nearly killed her."

"No, you didn't. She was never in any danger. And even if she had swallowed the necklace and ring, much worse things could have happened. She could have swallowed bathroom cleaner, someone's medication, drugs. Anything. Kids put stuff in their mouths. It's why you have to be so cautious."

With each item she ticked off on her fingers, he felt his stomach roil. He didn't even know where Mavis kept the bathroom cleaner. But surely they had some. As for medications or drugs, he knew neither he nor Derek took illegal drugs or even prescription drugs regularly. But who knew what over-the-counter medicines they had lying around.

He vaguely remembered Tim from marketing talking about hiring a professional to baby-proof his house. At the time Dex had laughed his ass off. First thing in the morning, Dex was getting this guy's name from Tim. He needed professional help.

Lucy, however, didn't seem nearly as worried as she should be. She just continued chatting away.

"The important thing is, when you thought she'd swallowed the ring, you didn't panic."

He tossed back the rest of his drink. "Excuse me, but I'm afraid I did."

She crossed to stand beside him. "You were scared. Terrified maybe." She ran her hand up and down his bicep in a way that was surprisingly soothing. "Any parent would be scared under those circumstances. I know I was. But still you did the right thing. You took her straight to the hospital."

At her touch, he felt the anxiety begin to ease from his body, only to be replaced by a different kind of tension. Staring down into her wide green eyes, which were so full of reassurances, so full of trust, he wanted to believe he could be the kind of father she thought he was capable of being.

But that certainly wasn't all that he wanted.

There was a hell of a lot he didn't know about caring for a child. But there were things he did know. He knew sex was the best release after an intense experience. He knew how to make a woman groan with pleasure. He knew how to make her ache. And he certainly knew how to bury all of his self-doubts and recriminations in the pleasure he could find in a woman's body.

He raised his hand to brush a lock of bright-red hair from her cheek. "This must have been very hard on you, too."

She licked her lips nervously as her hand slowed, then stilled on his arm. "I'll be okay." As if she just realized she was touching him, she jerked her hand away. "But I'm tired and should—"

But he didn't let her retreat. Instead, he snatched her hand from midair and used it to pull her into his arms. "Don't. We both need this."

He pulled her to his chest, more roughly than he intended to. But she didn't protest when he lowered his mouth to hers and kissed her.

Nine

Her body melted against his, all soft curves and pliant woman. He tasted her need. Her passion. But also her fear and desperation. Her need for reassurances.

What surprised him was his own echoing emotions. She may have needed this, but so did he.

He lost himself in her touch. In the way her mouth opened under his lips and her tongue arched up to meet his. The way her hands clutched at him, burrowing into his hair. The way her breasts pressed into his chest, full and soft in contrast to her hardening nipples.

He stepped his feet between hers, forcing her legs wider apart. Her thighs parted, one calf creeping up the outside of his leg, her pelvis bumping against his erection.

Groaning as his desire spiraled, he pulled her even closer, plastering her body against him, sinking his fingers into the flesh of her buttocks. Her body felt so warm, so solid beneath his hands. So reassuringly feminine.

He pulled his mouth from hers to bury his face in her neck. She moaned, low in her throat as her head dropped back to give him access. Her skin was hot, replete with the scent of her, musky and filled with desire. Her desperate need called out to him, resonating with a pounding urgency. He backed her up, one step and then another, until they fell back together into the plush depths of the sofa.

In the moment their bodies were apart, her hands reached between them, tugging at the buttons of his shirt for one frustrating minute before abandoning them for the button and zipper of her jeans.

Still kissing her, he felt more than saw her tugging her own jeans down her hips and kicking her legs free. That was all the invitation he needed. A moment later, he buried his fingers deep into her heat. Her folds were moist and plump against his hand, pulsing with desire.

The feel of her, the heat of her, made his erection tighten and strain against his jeans, bucking to get free.

She arched and moaned against him. "Please, tell me you have a condom."

It took a moment for her words to register. When they finally did, he nearly cursed. A condom was the last thing on his mind. Still, he groped for his jeans, found the foil packet he knew was in his wallet and a moment later he was back in her arms.

The sight of her there on the sofa, shirt unbuttoned to reveal her perfect breasts still encased in her pale pink bra, her creamy thighs parted, nearly sent him over the edge.

She opened her arms to him, urgency writ clearly on her face, but he forced himself to slow down. "No. Not yet."

With excruciating slowness, he unclasped her bra then peeled away the silken fabric to reveal breasts that were firm and lush, nipples peaked and darkened with desire.

He'd never seen more perfect breasts. But as tempting as they were, her faint gasp of anticipation was even more erotic. The fervency of her passion turned him on in a way no other woman ever had.

With hands that nearly trembled, he stripped off her remaining clothes, relishing every inch of her body as it was revealed.

A moment later, he buried himself in her. He lost himself in the heat and energy of her body. In the thrusting of her hips and desperate clutching of her hands. In the soft moans of pleasure resonating in her chest.

She wrapped her legs around his waist and arched further into him. Her eagerness only turned him on more. God, she was amazing.

This wasn't the practiced seduction he'd imagined. On his part, there was no skill. No pretense. No art.

Just lust and exquisite passion.

And Lucy.

She was everywhere. She was pounding through his mind, thundering through his blood.

With every stroke of his body, his pleasure built until he could feel nothing but the heat of her body, the clenching of her muscles around him, the spasm of her climax. Until it seemed as if her very soul was imprinted on him.

As his own climax rocketed through him, he knew he'd never forget that moment. Never forget her.

How had he ever forgotten her?

Waves of pleasure still undulated through her body. Dex, heavy and warm, lay on top of her, their bodies still intimately joined. And already she was having doubts.

Okay, not doubts, exactly. More like a full-fledged onslaught of panic.

One part of her—the logical, intelligent part that had guided every decision she'd made since she was eleven—had launched into reprimand mode.

What were you thinking?

You don't sleep with men you barely know. And this wasn't just any virtual stranger, either. This was Dex. Isabella's father. You shouldn't even be alone with him. You've lied to him. Deceived him. This is a man who could crush you like a bug if he finds out.

And by sleeping with him, she'd greatly increased the risk that he *would* find out. After all, he'd slept with Jewel. Sensual, exotic Jewel, who knew how to tempt and entice a man beyond endurance.

Lucy had none of Jewel's skills in bed and only a tiny fraction of her experience. Was there any chance at all that Dex wouldn't notice the woman he'd had sex with just now was nothing like the woman he'd slept with fourteen months ago?

She held her breath, waiting for him to comment on the differences, praying that he'd chalk it up to the high emotions of the evening. And all the while, her mental debate continued.

This man isn't just some heartless automaton, the emotional side of her argued. *He was just as worried as I was this evening. Surely it was natural to take comfort in each other.*

Natural? It was convenient, that's what it was. And what now? How many more times in the next few weeks will it be natural to seek comfort in sex again? How many more times will you make that mistake? And how much harder will it be now to take Isabella and leave when the time comes?

Ah, it always came back to that, didn't it? Back to her pledge to do whatever it took to get Isabella back.

But what if she wasn't right? Who was to say taking Isabella away from Dex was the right thing to do?

Sure, when she'd thought he *was* nothing more than a heartless automaton, doing everything in her power to get custody of Isabella had made sense. It had been justified. But she no longer believed that. As of tonight, she knew he cared about Isabella.

Lucy thought briefly of the diamond ring necklace still tucked safely in her purse. Obviously, giving his daughter a diamond ring wasn't a romantic gesture, but it was a gesture of some kind. It showed how much Isabella meant to him, almost as much as his panic had when he'd thought she was in danger. Just more proof that he'd grown to care for Isabella.

Maybe as much as she did.

So what gave her the right to decide what was best for any of them?

She was so lost in her mental debate that she barely noticed when he rolled off her and left for the bathroom. He returned a few minutes later with a glass of water for her. She took it from him without meeting his eyes.

"Where did you go?" he asked.

She looked up at him in surprise at his question. "What?"

"One minute there was a passionate woman in my arms." He pulled on his jeans as he spoke. "The next it's like you're not even here."

She turned her back on him, suddenly embarrassed by the intimacy of the situation. She placed her glass on the table, then pulled on her own jeans before turning back to face him. But instead of answering his question, she posed one of her own.

"You're not going to give me custody of Isabella, are you?"

"Sole custody?"

"Yes." Her breath caught in her chest as she waited for

his answer, even though she already knew what it would be. It all came down to this. Sex aside, emotions aside, this was the issue that stood between them.

"No. Not sole custody."

"No matter what I do? No matter how good a mother I prove myself to be? You won't even consider it, will you?"

She gazed into his eyes as she spoke, willing him to see her desperation. Her need.

Forcing herself to really see him as well. Not as just the man who could take Isabella away from her. Not as just some rich man with more money than heart.

As a father. As a man who had sought and given comfort. Not to mention tremendous pleasure.

Oh, it might be all too easy to demonize him. To pretend he didn't have any needs or rights for her to consider.

But wasn't it bad enough that she'd been lying to him? Did she really need to continue lying to herself as well?

Grief welled in her chest, forcing her to turn away from him.

He must have seen the desperation in her gaze, because he quickly closed the distance between them. Tenderly, he cupped her cheek, tilting her head up to his.

"This isn't about how good a mother you are," Dex said. "This is about what's best for Izzie. I don't doubt you're the best mother for her. But she needs a father, too."

Somehow his use of the nickname, Izzie, was like a stab in her heart. Like suddenly he had a piece of Isabella that she didn't. A piece that she'd never get back. She protested automatically. "But—"

"There are lots of single mothers out there who would disagree with me, I'm sure. But you don't have to do this alone. Besides, I have financial resources you couldn't hope to match."

"Money?" she asked incredulously, jerking away from his touch. Why had she brought this up now? Why couldn't she have just enjoyed lying in his arms? Instead, she'd brought up the one subject guaranteed to drive a wedge between them. "You're making this about money?"

"I'm just being honest."

"By pointing out that if it came down to a court battle, you would win by the sheer size of your wallet?"

"That's not what I meant. You know as well as I do that raising a child is expensive."

"Ah." She held up her palm to silence him. He didn't need to go on, she could do that for him. "I suppose you're going to point out that if you raise Isabella, she'll have the best of everything. The best schools, the best clothes, the best education."

"And you're…" he interrupted her, "…undoubtedly going to point out that there's more to life than material wealth."

Of course, that was what she was going to say. But in truth she couldn't deny that money made things easier. Instead, she sank to the edge of the sofa and rested her elbows on her knees, as resignation settled over her.

Growing up, her own family had been lower-middle class, not poor by any means, but well out of the league of most of the families in their upper-middle-class school district.

Her father had done what he could to provide for them—he'd made sure they got an excellent education—but she remembered all too well the yearning for nicer things, for the clothes and baubles other girls wore. Clothes were the least of it, of course. She would have been thrilled with the occasional warm word of encouragement from her father. But in lieu of that, there had been material things that would have made her feel less like an outsider. Less pitiable, perhaps.

"You're right, of course. Money isn't everything, but it does help."

Since she'd had the love of neither a mother nor a father, she'd simply held her head high, worn her shabby clothes with all the dignity she could muster and made sure that no one had had the chance to feel sorry for her. Not for anything she had control over, at least. She hadn't asked for handouts. She hadn't complained. And she had never, ever let anyone know that *she* knew she was second-class.

She wanted better than that for Isabella. How could she not?

Standing, she wrapped her arms around her waist and crossed to the massive fireplace at the far end of the room. On this warm spring night, it was empty, of course, except for an artfully arranged triad of pillar candles. "I was accepted to Brown and Princeton, but my dad didn't have the money to send me to either."

"Financial aid," he pointed out, ignoring the apparent non sequitur.

"Naturally I qualified, but I still would have been left with a mountain of debt." She chuckled, making light of the decision that had broken her heart at eighteen. "And I was far too practical to take that on. Not when I had a perfectly good scholarship from the University of Texas." She turned back to him. "So you see I know all too well that money *does* matter. I'm not saying it doesn't. Just that it's not everything."

"I couldn't agree more. And I would never dream of trying to raise Izzie all on my own. You're her mother. She needs you. She's going to continue to need you her whole life. I won't give you sole custody, but I'd never dream of taking her away from you altogether."

Oh, but he would.

Just as soon as he found out she wasn't really Isabella's mother, he'd do everything in his power to make sure she never saw Isabella again.

And now, she was beginning to realize, that wasn't the only heartbreak in her future. Never seeing Isabella again would be bad enough. But of course she'd lose Dex as well. Even if she could survive the one, could she survive the other?

Ten

Dex spent the following day hounding Quinn about Lucy. Unfortunately, Quinn had found out nothing Dex didn't already know. By all appearances, Lucy Alwin was a model citizen. She paid her taxes, earned a comfortable income and returned her library books on time. She'd never gotten so much as a speeding ticket. Nothing in her past or present raised a single red flag.

It was beginning to look as if she'd made only two mistakes in her whole life. Sleeping with him and abandoning Isabella on his doorstep. He'd been complicit in the first, so he could hardly blame her for that. As for why she'd abandoned Isabella, that was still a mystery.

But one thing was obvious. Since he and Derek had never reported that incident to the authorities, and since Lucy's record was otherwise squeaky-clean, he would have a hell of a time convincing a judge Lucy was an unfit mother.

If he wanted to go that route, that was.

But dragging Lucy and Isabella through a nasty court battle was no longer something he could imagine doing. Which left him with only one option. If he wanted custody of Isabella, he was going to have to marry Lucy.

Dex's neighborhood was not the kind of place where salesman traveled door to door hawking their goods. So the chime of the doorbell ringing at two o'clock in the afternoon, mere moments after she'd put Isabella down for her nap, definitely took Lucy by surprise.

As she walked to the front door she made a mental list of who could possibly be on the other side. Girl Scouts selling Thin Mints? Ed McMahon with a giant check? That skinny chick from *What Not to Wear*, there to overhaul Lucy's wardrobe?

She swung open the heavy mahogany door to reveal a tall woman, not quite as thin as the *What Not to Wear* woman, but darn close. The similarity was accented by the bulky, black garment bag she held in her hand. The woman's dishwater-blond hair was pulled back in a tight cinch, which either caused or exaggerated her pinched expression, Lucy wasn't sure which. Either way, Lucy got the distinct impression that this woman did not want to be there.

"May I help you?" Lucy hesitated to ask the question, in case it pissed off the ice queen even more.

"Raina Huffman." She held out her hand, but the handshake was anything but warm. Then she breezed through the door without waiting to be invited in. "I'm Mr. Messina's assistant. Mr. Derek Messina's assistant, that is. Dex sent me to bring you these."

Raina held out the garment bag, at which Lucy stared blankly.

"His dry cleaning?" she asked flatly.

"No." There was an exasperated eye roll in Raina's tone that she somehow managed to convey while keeping her expression carefully blank. "This is a collection of outfits Dex thought might be appropriate for you to wear to tonight's gala event."

"Oh…"

When Lucy didn't rush to take the bag from Raina, she draped it over the back of the sofa. "I've included—"

"What gala event?"

"Tonight Messina Diamonds Dallas is hosting a black-tie reception to celebrate the opening of their Antwerp office. Dex thought you should attend. He told me to make sure you had an appropriate gown and suggested you might like to have your hair and makeup done for the event."

"Ah. That gala event," she snapped peevishly. Dex had mentioned a couple of days ago that he had a business function to attend that night. And now he was ordering her to attend, too. Typical Messina autocracy. "Well, you can just tell him that you tried, but that I can't attend any event, gala or otherwise, appropriate clothes or no appropriate clothes. I have Isabella to look after. I can't leave her here alone."

"That has been arranged as well. I've hired a very reputable babysitting service. They'll be sending someone over shortly." Raina glanced at her watch. "A driver will be here to take you to your hair appointment in an hour. Also, I would suggest a slightly more—" her gaze lingered unpleasantly on Lucy's Jewel-inspired bright red hair "—conservative hairstyle."

Irritation spiked through Lucy, despite the fact that she didn't like the garish red of her hair any more than Raina appeared to. She didn't know who she was more annoyed with: Raina for judging her with such disdain after an acquaintance of less than ten minutes, or Dex for siccing this woman on her.

Okay, Lucy told herself. *Don't take this out on her. Maybe she's just doing her job. Or has an enormous stick shoved up her butt.*

All but biting her tongue, she ignored Raina's "suggestion" and crossed the room to the garment bag, curious what the ice princess would deem appropriate cocktail wear. A starchy Victorian gown, perhaps?

The corner of the bag bore the embossed logo of an exclusive retail shop. The kind of place Lucy could barely afford to drive past, let alone shop at. Just her luck. The only time in her life she'd ever even touch a dress from that shop and it had been picked out by Ms. Congeniality.

However, when she unzipped the bag, a soft gasp of surprise slipped out unbidden. The first dress inside was a deep teal silk with a ruched bodice and a long, flowing skirt.

"You don't like it."

"No, I—" She reached out a tentative hand to touch the dress, only to pull back, all too aware of the baby drool that likely lingered on her fingers. "It's gorgeous. You picked it out?"

She couldn't keep the surprise from her voice and Raina frowned in response to it.

"There are three dresses. One of the other ones may be more to your liking."

"No. This is beautiful. But is the reception really this formal?"

Raina stiffened. "This isn't my first reception at Messina Diamonds. I picked out what I thought would be appropriate and—"

Great. She'd offended her again. Lucy held up a hand

to halt Raina's sputtering. "Oh, I trust you. It's just the last time I wore a dress this fancy, Jake, my prom date, drank too much and puked all over it at three in the morning."

"I'm sure he did."

"It's a beautiful dress," Lucy said sincerely, since humor didn't seem to be working at softening Raina up. "You have excellent taste." Lucy looked up to find Raina scowling, clearly annoyed by the compliment. "Why do I get the feeling you don't like me very much?"

Raina blinked in surprise, then pressed her lips together. "I don't know what you mean."

"Sure you do. You're going to get a crick in your neck if you look any farther down your nose at me. Now, don't get me wrong, I can understand your being annoyed that Dex sent you to be my personal shopper—that would annoy anyone." She cocked her head to the side, studying the other woman, trying to see beyond the cool haughtiness. "But this is more than that. You really don't like me."

"Well, if you must know, Jewel…" Raina put a little sneer into the word *Jewel* "…Dex may not remember your stint working at Messina Diamonds, but I do."

"Oh." Lucy bit down on her lip, trying to hide her distress. She'd been so focused on convincing Dex she was the woman he'd slept with, she'd completely forgotten that Jewel worked for Messina Diamonds at one point. It had never occurred to her she might have to convince anyone else she was Jewel. Having a fellow employee pop up who remembered Jewel from her days there was completely unexpected.

Lucy fought the urge to defend her sister. What could she possibly say, when she had no idea what history this woman shared with Jewel?

Since Raina obviously expected some kind of response,

Lucy shrugged and went for something vague. "I guess I wasn't an ideal employee."

"You guess? Dressing inappropriately, flirting outrageously. Constantly throwing yourself at—"

But Raina stopped herself. Again her cheeks flushed and her gaze darted away from Lucy's. Apparently, she'd said far more than she'd intended.

Suddenly, Raina's attitude began to make sense. Her voice had been laced with scorn, but Lucy could tell it hid a deeper, darker emotion. Jealousy.

And this, she realized, was what it was actually like to be Jewel. Jewel's sexuality had always been her greatest strength and her greatest weakness. She used it to lure men in and keep women at arm's length.

"Ah. So you don't like me because I was always throwing myself at Dex?"

"Not Dex. Derek." Raina frowned at Lucy's slipup, but then continued fiercely, "But Derek would never sleep with an employee."

Derek? Jewel had been throwing herself at Derek?

Lucy recovered quickly. "Which is why I threw myself at Dex. That's what I meant."

The twisted machinations of Jewel's love life were becoming more and more...well, twisted. And yet, somehow, it all made sense. Jewel had a long history of developing crushes on unattainable men. After all, a skilled hunter isn't satisfied hunting deer. Sooner or later, she'll give in to the lure of big game.

Derek must have posed quite the challenge. Undoubtedly, the more he'd resisted, the more determined Jewel had become. She'd probably thrown herself at him the whole time she'd worked at Messina Diamonds. When he hadn't nibbled, she'd set her cap on Dex instead.

And all the while, there was poor Raina, who obviously cared about Derek, though she was doing an admirable job of hiding it. But Lucy knew the signs well. The jealousy, the fierce protectiveness, the way her voice thickened when she said his name.

Well, if Jewel had a long history of manipulating men, Lucy had an equally long history of smoothing over her sister's mistakes.

"Raina, I'm sorry." Since the other woman was standing only a short distance away, Lucy reached for Raina's arm. "I didn't know you were in love with him."

Raina jerked away. "I'm not in love with him."

But the vehemence of her response and the heightened color in her cheeks proved her a liar.

And Lucy knew all too well what it felt like to have someone she was interested in lured away by her sister's innate sensual appeal.

"If it makes you feel any better," Lucy pointed out, "he didn't sleep with me, either. Derek really wouldn't sleep with an employee."

"Really?" A glimmer of something like hope flashed in Raina's eyes, but there was caution there as well.

Lucy certainly couldn't blame Raina for not trusting a gesture of friendship from someone like Jewel. However, she felt too much kinship with Raina to not try. After all, how many times in her own life had men overlooked her because she lacked Jewel's overt sensuality? How many broken hearts had she nursed while watching her sister ride off in the front seat with some guy Lucy had secretly had a crush on?

Too many. She knew all too well that it was no fun.

And in some weird way, wasn't that what was happening all over again? Here she was, well on the way to losing her heart to Dex and the only reason he even knew she existed was because he thought she was Jewel.

She was as much a victim of Jewel's power over men as Raina was. Besides, she could certainly use a friend tonight at this gala event she'd been ordered to attend. That alone was reason enough to extend the olive branch again.

"Can I assume you're going to this reception, too?" she asked Raina, who nodded. "Well, it certainly wasn't very nice of him to send you here to do his dirty work when you probably need to be getting ready, also."

Raina shrugged in a gesture of beleaguered resignation. "I'm Derek's go-to girl. And sometimes Dex's by proximity. I do what they need me to do."

"Gawd, I hope they pay you bundles to do it."

Finally, a smile cracked through Raina's icy facade. "Well, at least there's that."

Lucy laughed as inspiration struck. "Look, if Dex is footing the bill for this spa afternoon thing, why don't you come with me? I'd be thrilled to have someone tackle this mess I've made of my hair…" The garish red favored by Jewel gave her a fright every time she looked in the mirror. "But I certainly don't need a manicure or a pedicure. It'll be a girl's afternoon out."

In the end, they both got their nails done. The few occasions when Lucy had had a manicure and pedicure, she'd just gone to the Walk-Ins Welcome nail salon in the strip mall near her condo. She'd never been to a full-service day spa before. Between the soft classical music, the dimmed lights, the massage chair and the fragrant herbal tea, it was all Lucy could do not to fall asleep while getting her hair dyed.

Four hours later, she emerged from the cocoon of the salon like a pampered and rested butterfly. Two hours after that, she found herself swathed in shimmering teal silk, seated next to Raina in the back of the limo Dex had sent to pick her up, grateful she wasn't having to navigate the downtown Dallas traffic.

Raina, who'd been thawing all afternoon, looked at her appraisingly. "You look good with that hair color."

"I do?" Remarkably, the hairdresser had picked a shade very close to her own natural brown. He'd added a few auburn highlights and trimmed up the shaggy bob, which had left Lucy feeling less like a pale imitation of Jewel and rather like a slightly more glamorous version of herself. She smiled. "Maybe I'll keep it like this."

"You should." And then Raina hesitated, biting her lip before adding, "You're not at all like I thought you were."

"Yeah. I'm getting that a lot lately," she muttered wryly. When Raina raised her eyebrows in question, Lucy added, "I guess becoming a mom has really changed me."

"I can see that. I'm the oldest of five. Dealing with the little ones either makes you crazy or makes you a better person. Usually both."

Lucy chuckled, but it felt forced. She really liked Raina and, in the end, she was yet another person Lucy was lying to. Imagining how Raina would respond when she found out the truth—as she inevitably would—made Lucy squirm. More lies. More deception. And it was getting harder and harder to tell herself her motives were pure.

Luckily, she was saved from having to come up with an answer as the limo pulled to a halt in front of the towering building that housed Messina Diamonds. Even though she'd lived in Dallas for most of her life, she'd never really been downtown at night. Downtown Dallas wasn't alive at night like Chicago or Manhattan. The streets were well lit, but empty of pedestrians. There was road traffic, but no crowds spilling out from restaurants or bars. However, this swath of downtown was aglow. Cars lined up before the building, elegantly dressed men and women stepping from limos like glitterati.

Lucy double-checked to make sure she had her evening clutch before climbing out of the limo. That morning, she'd dropped by the jewelry store to have Dex's ring cleaned. She hadn't felt comfortable leaving the ring at the house, so she'd been carrying it around in its velvet jewelry box until she could give it back to Dex.

By the time they made it up to the Messina Diamonds offices on the fifteenth floor, Lucy was feeling decidedly outclassed, even in her stunning teal gown. She'd never even ridden in a limo before tonight, let alone attended a gala event. For her, a big night out was getting popcorn at the movies. She didn't belong in this elevator full of sparkling, laughing people. What could she possibly have in common with any of them? As the elevator doors opened, Raina placed a hand on Lucy's arm.

"Take a deep breath," Raina murmured. "It'll help you calm down."

"That obvious, huh?"

"You look ready to pass out."

"Ah, but the question is—" Lucy smoothed her hands down over her hips as she spoke "—does peaked go with formal wear?"

Raina chuckled under her breath. "Just remember, no one here is any better than you, no matter how they may act. Besides, you're the only woman here tonight personally invited by Dex."

"Invited? Ordered was more like it," Lucy grumbled.

"Just try to have fun."

As Raina spoke, the crowd parted and Lucy got her first

glimpse of Dex's office. The Messina Diamonds offices were both more and less impressive than she'd expected.

Less, because she somehow thought they'd be bigger. The office took up a modest six floors of a downtown sky-scraper. Only six. Which seemed tiny for a multi-billion-dollar business. Of course, they also had offices in Toronto, New York and Antwerp.

At least the logo etched in the massive wall of glass that faced Lucy when she exited the elevator on the fifteenth floor said so. The words *Messina Diamonds* arched across the glass, and underneath was the image of a diamond ring laying on its side, the diamond cut in a distinctive elongated oval. In smaller letters underneath that the four cities were listed.

She stared at the image of the ring for a long moment. "I know that ring."

"The legendary Messina family diamond." Raina nodded.

"Legendary?"

"Of course." Raina pushed open the heavy glass door and led the way into the lobby. "That's the first diamond dis-covered by Derek and Dex's father. The elder Mr. Messina, I mean. By the time the diamond mine was operational, their mother had already passed away. But Mr. Messina had the diamond set in a ring for her anyway because she's the only woman he ever loved." A hint of wistfulness had crept into Raina's voice, revealing the romanticism she tried so hard to hide. "He carried it with him until the day he died."

"And then he gave it to Dex," Lucy murmured as her heart sank under the weight of the story.

So it wasn't just any ring Dex had given to Isabella. Not just a trinket a diamond magnate would thoughtlessly bestow on his child. This was a ring of great importance to Dex.

Raina's head whipped around and stared at Lucy. "How did you know that?"

"Not because he gave it to me, if that's what you're worried about." She had to work to keep her own hint of wistfulness from her voice. Her disappointment was too illogical to share with someone else.

Raina flushed. "I wasn't worried, I just…"

"Ah. You thought I might abscond with the family heirloom?"

"It's not that. I was just surprised. Mr. Messina gave it to Dex on his deathbed. He wanted him to give it to the love of *his* life."

"Which explains why he gave it to Isabella."

Raina's expression softened. "To Isabella? That's charming."

"Yes. It is."

Dex really loved Isabella. And the fact that he'd given the ring to her was a sign he'd really welcomed her into his heart.

She should be thrilled. So why did the smile plastered on her face feel like it was cracking around the edges?

Surely not because she was jealous? That was absurd. It wasn't as if she wanted Dex to love her. Was it?

Eleven

"Champagne?"

"Hmm?" For a second, Lucy stared blankly at Raina, who had snagged a waiter wandering by with a tray of champagne flutes.

"Or there's an open bar if you'd prefer wine."

"No. Champagne's great." And maybe if she sounded excited enough about it, Raina would even believe her.

The reception was being held in the lobby of Messina Diamonds offices, with the open bar set up in one corner and tables of appetizers along the walls. However, the crowd of tuxedoed men and elegant women had spilled out to the elevator bay and beyond the lobby to the conference rooms.

Though she wouldn't have thought the lobby of a business was the perfect place to hold such a glamorous event, somehow it seemed appropriate. Everything about the lobby spoke of austere elegance—frosted glass, brushed metal and creamy, golden marble. The room was crescent-shaped, with the glass wall facing the elevator forming the shorter side, and the opposite wall arcing from corner to corner in a broad arch.

The center of that wall also bore the Messina Diamonds logo. On either side of it, in two wide columns of foot-high letters, was printed "The Story of Randolph Messina."

"I can give you the nickel tour if you'd like?" Raina asked.

"Maybe later. You don't have to babysit me all evening." Even in the short time they'd been there, several people had nodded at Raina in greeting. "I'll be fine here. I'm just going to…" Lucy let her words trail off as she pointed to the paragraphs printed on the wall.

After a few minutes of convincing, Raina wandered off to work the room, leaving Lucy to read about Messina Diamonds. She felt slightly voyeuristic, but excused the feeling by telling herself that—if Dex had anything to do with it—Isabella would someday be heir to this company. Besides, it wasn't as if Dex had been exactly forthcoming about his family history.

Of course, her curiosity was ridiculous. She knew that. Despite the single night of breathtaking passion they'd shared, nothing had changed. He still wanted Isabella. She was still lying to him. They still had no future. So why did her heart ache a little at the idea of losing him? Surely she hadn't gone and done something really stupid, like fall in… No. Even she wasn't that dumb. No, if anything, she was merely vulnerable to his charisma. Whatever she was feeling was a temporary glitch in her emotions. Nothing more.

Forcing her attention away from her troublesome feelings and back to the real world, she scanned the text before turning her attention to the picture inset into the left column of text. The black-and-white photo of a stocky, rough-looking man in a cowboy hat with his arm around a willowy woman with flowing long hair. He indeed looked like he'd stepped out of a gold mine from 1849. She, however, looked like she'd stepped off a runway in Paris.

Dex had obviously gotten his height from his mother's side, but she could see his father in the curve of his lips and the shape of his eyes. And unless she was mistaken, Randolph's eyes would be the same piercing blue-gray as Isabella's.

"There's a better picture of them upstairs."

Lucy spun around to see Dex with his elbow propped on the receptionist's desk. Like all the men she'd seen tonight, he was dressed in a tux. Somehow on him, it looked even more impressive. It might have been the breadth of his shoulders or the clean lines of the tux, which was obviously custom-made. Or perhaps just the casual confidence with which he stood there. Dex may pretend he was just an ordinary guy, and until tonight she'd been fooled, but he was obviously as much in his element here as he was back at the house playing on the floor with Isabella or sitting by the pool drinking a Shiner.

"You look lovely."

The appreciative gleam in his gaze warmed her to the core, reminding her of the intimacy they'd shared. She blushed, remembering, and had to force herself to respond. She ran a hand down the front of her gown. "Raina has excellent taste."

"I wasn't talking about the dress."

Her blush deepened at his compliment and she found herself at a loss for words. *You look better in a tux than James Bond* were the words that popped into her head.

After a moment, he took pity on her and asked, "Would you like to come up and see the rest of the offices?"

"Actually, I've been enjoying the story."

Dex grimaced. "That was the PR department's idea."

"It sounds like your dad was a bit of a character."

"He was the last of a dying breed."

Lucy looked sharply at Dex. "And there's no pride in your voice when you say that."

He looked a little surprised at her observation. "No. I suppose not."

"And yet," she pointed out, "it says here he was devoted to your mother and to his family. That he was a brilliant geologist."

"That's the work of the PR people again. 'Devoted to his family' merely means he dragged us all over South America when we were kids. 'Brilliant geologist' really means headstrong and foolhardy. He believed he'd find diamonds in Canada and no one else could convince him otherwise."

"But he was right."

"In the end, yes he was."

Dex didn't continue and she guessed there was a lot he wasn't telling her. Resentment, perhaps, at being "dragged all over South America" as a kid? Or perhaps just a troubled relationship with his headstrong and foolhardy father?

"You don't talk much about your family."

"You haven't said much about yours, either."

"True enough." She shrugged and then rattled off the highlights. "Raised by a single dad. Mom left when we were young. I have one sister." Better to be as vague about that as possible. "Dad was a CPA," she added quickly.

"You must have gotten your love of numbers from him."

"My love of—" Then she broke off with a chuckle. "Oh, I see. Because I'm an actuary. Um. No. Sorry, not from him." If her father had loved his job, he certainly hadn't let her see it. He hadn't passed a love of anything on to his children. Doing so would have required showing too much emotion.

Feeling suddenly self-conscious—as if she'd given away far more than she'd intended—she rushed on. "No. The whole actuary gig was just more of me being practical. I was always good in math. And there are lots of scholarships and job opportunities in that field. Especially if you're a woman."

"You remind me of my mother."

When she looked up at him in surprise, an odd expression crossed his face, giving her the impression he hadn't meant to say that aloud.

"That sounds like something that could have been a compliment, but wasn't," she observed.

"Always so practical. Always doing the right thing. Making sacrifices for other people."

"Those aren't bad qualities."

"They are if they keep you from doing what you really want with your life."

Lucy returned her attention to the photo on the wall, to the smiling faces of the couple. Randolph was smiling into the camera, but the woman, Sara, had her head cocked just slightly toward her husband. The expression on her face, the tilt of her lips, suggested she was seconds away from a full-blown chuckle, as if her husband had said something outrageously funny mere seconds before the picture had been taken.

Nothing in her expression bespoke a woman unhappy with her choices.

"Who's to say she wasn't doing exactly what she wanted to do?"

"Trust me, prospecting for gold and diamonds isn't the

glamorous work you might imagine it to be." A note of bitterness crept into his voice. "Prospectors travel to crappy little towns in the middle of nowhere. That's if there is a town. Typically, there are no hotels. No shops. More often than not, there isn't even any running water. Diamond mines aren't found in New York City half a block away from the Ritz-Carlton."

"I never said they were."

"It's hard work. Under brutal conditions. No one deserves to live like that."

"Are you talking about why you think your mother was unhappy or why you were unhappy?"

The expression that flickered across his face was positively chilly. But it was gone in an instant, replaced by cool disinterest.

"Oh, I get it now."

"Get what?"

"All those years of rebellious behavior that you pretend to be so proud of."

He appeared to be gritting his teeth, "I'm not proud of—"

"Well, of course not. Because you're not really a rebel. The media portrays you like the renegade of the Messina family. But that's not it at all. You didn't travel around the world, refusing to accept a position at Messina Diamonds because you're some kind of renegade. You know why you did it?"

"I'm sure you're going to tell me."

She ignored his obvious annoyance. "You did it to get back at your father and brother. On the one hand, for the first time in your life you had control over where you lived and what you did. After years of being dragged all over the world—your words, not mine—you probably wanted to settle down in one place. Put down some roots. But by then,

Messina Diamonds was taking off. Your father needed you to settle into the family business. So you were torn between the desire to do what you wanted and the compulsion to disappoint your father. After all, he'd disappointed you for so many years. So you made yourself into the rebel loner. Traveling all over the world, keeping everyone at arm's length. All to protect yourself."

She felt a surge of triumph at her explanation. For an instant it even seemed like maybe she understood him. He, however, didn't give even a flicker of a response. In fact, he spoke as if she hadn't said a word.

"Why don't I show you the rest of the office." He placed a hand at the small of her back and guided her to the doors behind the receptionist desk.

Wow. Wasn't that interesting?

Apparently, he had a nice big tender spot where his childhood was concerned and she'd just trampled all over it.

As soon as they were out of earshot of the other partygoers, she pulled away from him. "Look, Dex, I didn't mean to offend you."

He raked her face with a dispassionate gaze. "I'm not offended." With one hand shoved firmly in his pocket, he gestured broadly with the other one. "These offices—"

"Excuse me, but you obviously are offended." When he turned back to face her, she saw that his jaw was clenched, his eyes shuttered. "You've clearly got this enormous Do Not Disturb sign right where your childhood memories should be and—"

"Don't analyze me."

She held up her hands in acquiescence. "Trust me, I'm not *trying* to. It doesn't take much effort to see that you still resent your parents for mistakes they—"

"The word *mistake* implies 'accident.' When you take

your kids out of school and drag them halfway across the continent every time you want to dig in the dirt, that's not a mistake. That's a decision."

"Okay, so maybe your parents made some poor decisions." She gentled her tone. "You will, too, someday. All parents do."

"No," he said quietly but with firm finality. "Parents should do what's right for their child. Not just what they want, but what their child needs." With that, he turned his back on her and gestured toward a wall of cubicles to his left. "These offices belong to the junior researchers…"

Just like that, he continued with his tour of the office like she'd never even brought up the subject. And here she thought she had issues with her own childhood.

Of course, she did have issues—maybe everyone did. But she worked to overcome them. To find success and happiness in life despite the rough patches of youth.

In recent years, she and her father had come to a kind of peace in their relationship. And until this recent debacle, she'd have said she and Jewel were closer than they'd ever been. And she had Isabella. Her last, best hope to have the kind of family she'd always dreamed of.

But Dex?

He seemed closed off from everyone in his family. If he had any fond memories of his childhood, he sure wasn't sharing them with her.

Which, she supposed, wasn't surprising.

After all, what connection did they really share? They'd lived in the same house for a while and had had sex once. Well, twice, if you looked at it from his point of view.

Yes, they had Isabella in common, but that was it.

It was time she faced facts. He may be ready to let Isabella into his heart, but he was keeping that door firmly closed to her.

Twelve

Lucy barely paid attention to the tour she received of Messina Diamonds' six floors of offices. It was much as she expected: cubicles, offices, hundreds—if not thousands—of geological maps rolled up and stored, taped down to tables, tacked to walls. Most of the research and development was out of this office, Dex had explained.

He talked to her about the process of looking for diamonds, where they thought the next big find would come from, how long they estimated the mines would stay in production. And he did it all with a cool efficiency that bordered on impatience. Blah de blah, blah, blah. He told her nothing she *wanted* to know.

All of that information he kept firmly under wraps.

From what she'd read, she gathered his one true childhood home had been in Dallas. Was that why Messina Diamonds still had an office here? And if he had no fond memories of his childhood, why did he still live here? Why not in Toronto, New York or Antwerp?

But Dex didn't answer any of those questions. Geesh, he didn't even give her time to ask them. Her tour of Messina Diamonds was like a military strike. Fast, precise and a little chilling.

And just when her patience was about up, he ushered her into a spacious corner office with breathtaking views of the city. Unlike the other rooms she'd toured, this one was warm and inviting. The two walls not made up of windows were wood paneled. Centered in each of the shadow-box panels was a framed photo of his family. An oversized mahogany desk dominated the room, flanked on either side by dark leather chairs. Stacks of papers and folders littered one wing of the desk.

The overall effect was elegancy tempered by a sort of cozy clutter. It was a pleasantly intimate glimpse of his everyday life.

"So, this is your office," she murmured.

To her surprise, Dex turned around. "No. Actually, this is Derek's office."

"Oh." And if that wasn't enough to deflate what little enthusiasm she'd had for the tour, she didn't know what was.

"Have a seat."

Why had she even come here? she wondered as she lowered herself to the cushy leather wingback.

She'd never felt more out of place and she couldn't help wondering if this tour had been designed to impress or intimidate.

"If it's not your office, why are we even here?"

"Because of this." Dex turned to one of the larger framed photos of his family.

But before she could even glimpse the picture, he swung the frame away from the wall to reveal a wall safe.

"Oh." She sank back into her chair. "How exciting."

Why wouldn't he tell her something? Anything about his past? And why was she so desperate to know? But she knew the answer before her mind had even finished forming the question. Once he trusted her, once he opened up and told her a truth about himself, somehow it would be easier to tell him her truth. Tell him all about her charade and hope that it wasn't too late to ask for some forgiveness.

If Dex noticed her sarcasm, he didn't comment on it. He spun the dial on the wall safe a few times and then that door swung open, too.

From it, he pulled out a roll of black velvet. Not unlike the fabric used by the jeweler she'd visited earlier that day. She couldn't say why, but dread began to swirl in her stomach.

"For years now, Derek has been working toward vertical integration."

"I see," she murmured, even though she had no idea what that had to do with anything.

"Owning the diamond mines is certainly profitable. But he's been working to open a subsidiary of Messina Diamonds in Antwerp to handle the cutting, polishing and wholesale selling of our stones, as well."

This cold and formal discussion of business expansion actually relaxed her. He wasn't going to do something stupid. To him, diamonds weren't jewelry, they were business.

He crossed the desk in front of her, cleared a spot and unrolled the velvet. The rectangle of fabric was only slightly larger than a legal sheet of paper. A dozen diamonds glittered against the inky velvet.

Still, she couldn't quite stifle her gasp at the sight of all those rocks twinkling up at her. No woman in the world was immune to such beauty.

Unsure what he expected her to say, she said, "And these are from your mine?"

"They're the first batch to come out of the newly formed Messina Cutting House. I inspected them and brought them back during my recent trip to Belgium."

"I see." Though of course she didn't. His world was miles apart from her own. Diamonds, cutting houses, trips to Europe—it was all so foreign to her. She'd once been sent to corporate headquarters in Des Moines, but that was hardly the same thing.

"I personally inspected each of these stones. You won't find a finer diamond anywhere in the world. One of them could be yours."

A bark of panicky laughter escaped. "Not unless I wanted to clean out my savings and my retirement fund. Even then I'd be pushing it."

"That's not what I meant."

"That's what I was afraid of."

"I'm asking you—"

"Look, Dex—"

"—to be my wife. All you have to do is pick out the diamond for your ring."

That feeling of dread in her belly solidified into something hard and ugly. Something that felt a little like anger and a little like envy. But who was it she envied?

Dex had proposed to *her*. So why did it feel like it wasn't her he really wanted?

The anger was easier to put her finger on. All her life she'd waited for—dreamed of—this moment. The moment a man she genuinely cared about asked her to marry him. And here he had to go and ruin it by sucking out all the romance, all the warmth. He could have been asking to borrow a pencil for all the emotion he showed.

She stood up. "No, Dex. This is all wrong."

"Think about it, Lucy. I can give you everything you want."

"What do you know about what I want?" Her voice rose sharply in accusation.

In contrast, his voice came out smooth as butter. Soft and low, like the purring of a cat. "I know you. I know what you want."

"I'm sure you think you do." She cast a scornful glare at the diamonds on the desk between them.

"You want Izzie. You want a family. More important, you want to do the right thing for Izzie."

Her chest tightened as if he'd punched her in the solar plexus. She had to consciously suck in one breath after another before she could speak.

It was crazy, of course, how for an instant she was tempted.

She couldn't marry him. Every practical bone in her body knew the real reason she couldn't say yes. He didn't even know who she was. The lies she'd told stood between them like some huge, insurmountable obstacle.

And yet it was the impractical, romantic heart inside her that protested the loudest. Somehow, the biggest obstacle between them wasn't really the lies she'd told, but the fact that he didn't love her. Not even a little.

All her life, she'd been the practical one. It was a quality she nurtured in herself and admired in others. Yet here he was, being oh so practical. So *reasonable*. And every cell in her body recoiled at the thought.

"You're right. I do want a family. Of course I want a family. I want to be a mother to Isabella and to whatever brothers or sisters she has. But what you're describing isn't a family. It isn't a marriage. You're talking about a convenience."

"I'm talking about doing what's right for Izzie." He rounded the desk to stand before her, crowding her space, making her fight the urge to step back, to retreat. "Think about it. Izzie needs both her parents. How much easier will her life be if they live in the same house?"

"Easier? Because you could tell yourself you'd done the right thing by Isabella, but I'd be the one doing all the work. Yes, it would be easier for you, wouldn't it?"

"Easier for both of us. You could quit your job if you wanted to. You'd get to be with Izzie all the time. Both of us would." He raised his hand to her face and brushed her hair back in a sensual, seductive gesture. "And we know we're compatible."

For the briefest instant, she felt a burst of hope—that maybe, after all they'd been through, after the emotional turmoil of the past week-and-a-half, after they'd made love, that maybe he was starting to develop some tender feelings for her.

Maybe.

But then she saw the glint of sexual desire lighting his gaze.

Resignation threatened to smother her. He didn't mean they were emotionally compatible. He meant in bed, of course. And they were.

The sex had been incredible. But a marriage—a real marriage, the kind of marriage she wanted—wasn't based on sex and lies.

As if he sensed her wavering, he took her hands in his and added, "I know what you want most is Izzie. But surely there are other things you want. I'm a wealthy man, Lucy. I can give you whatever you want. Travel, cars, clothes, jewelry. Name it and it's yours."

"Ah." She stepped back, pulling her hands from his. "So that's what this is all about. You planned this all out, didn't you? From the moment Raina showed up on the doorstep. The dress. The trip to the day spa. Arriving via limousine at this glamorous affair. You created this perfect Cinderella evening, all so you could propose."

What a stupid, stupid man.

He said nothing, but the very corner of his mouth twitched upward, as if he was pleased with himself.

She laughed, for a moment genuinely amused by the absurdity of the situation. But when she spoke, her voice sounded brittle and hollow. "You know the thing men don't get about that story? Women don't love Cinderella only because Cinderella gets to dress up in fancy clothes and go to the ball. They love Cinderella because when the prince finds out that she's just a poor servant girl, he still loves her."

The beginnings of a frown settled on Dex's handsome face. As if he didn't quite get where she was going with the metaphor. So she made it easy for him.

"You want me to believe I can have anything I want. All I have to do is pick out a diamond. Any diamond in this room, right?"

Success glinted in his eyes. "Right."

"Any diamond—" she reached into her bag and pulled out the box from the jeweler "—except this one."

When she flipped open the box with her thumb, his gaze hardened. His lips compressed into a thin line, but he said nothing.

Bitterness laced her tone when she spoke. "Because this is the one diamond that means something to you, isn't it?"

Again, he said nothing and again she pressed on. "I'm not an idiot, Dex. I put two and two together. This is the ring from the logo. And Raina told me its history. It's the first diamond your father found. The ring your father had made for your mother, long after she'd passed away."

He didn't deny it, not that she expected him to.

He didn't meet her gaze, either, but turned away from her to face the bank of windows overlooking downtown. He shoved his hands into the pockets of his tuxedo pants. His back was a broad, impenetrable barrier.

Despite that, she kept talking, because her point was too important to let drop. Not for her, but for Isabella. And for Dex.

"You've worked so hard to push your family away, but this ring means something to you, Dex. That's why you gave it to Isabella the other night. You did it because you're starting to open up to her."

She waited for him to say something. Anything.

But his silence, his stubborn refusal to even turn and face her, hung between them, as insurmountable as her deception had ever been.

True, she couldn't marry him because of her lies. But it was funny, really, how *that* had become the least of the problems between them. It seemed a small thing compared to the fact that he didn't love her. That over and over again, he'd shut her out of his heart. That he was asking her only because she'd make the perfect long-term babysitter.

"Do you know what would happen if I did say yes?" she murmured. "Things would pretty much go back to how they were the first week Isabella and I lived with you. I would take care of her. I would love her heart and soul. And you would stop by to visit once every week or so. Yes, you'd be her father in the biological sense, and certainly in a financial sense, but in no other way.

"That's why I can't marry you. Well, actually—" a nervous little chuckle escaped "—there are a lot of reasons

I can't marry you. But the real reason is because you're asking for all the wrong reasons.

"If you married me, I'd take care of Isabella. Not just her physical needs, but her emotional ones, too. You'd have the perfect excuse to hold her at arm's length forever. All you'd have to do is pay for everything. You could have a daughter and a family, but you wouldn't have to care about either. Marrying me would let you push Isabella away, just like you've pushed away everyone else in your life."

She paused, holding her breath, praying he'd deny it.

When he didn't, she added, "But I can't let you do that to her. I can't let you do that to you."

Thirteen

Dex didn't turn around to watch Lucy leave. What would have been the point?

She was going. She would take Izzie with her. And he couldn't say that he blamed her.

As soon as she'd started babbling on about Cinderella, he'd known he'd lost. He'd made one fatal mistake. He'd appealed to her practical side.

What he hadn't realized until too late was that under all that practicality beat the heart of a romantic. Deep down, Lucy was the kind of woman who wanted it all. The whole sappy, romantic package.

Raina—a bit of a closet romantic herself—had told Lucy all about the damn ring at the reception and Lucy had fallen head over heels for the story.

He, on the other hand, had done everything in his power to avoid so much as walking past the damn PR display.

He'd read it exactly once, his stomach knotting with disgust. It was nothing more than a bit of revisionist history cooked up by the PR department in conjunction with an overpriced decorator.

What made for a charming press release did not make for an enjoyable childhood. The fact that his father eventually did strike gold—or, rather, diamonds—didn't make up for the fact that he'd dragged them across three continents, that they'd barely lived in the only home they'd ever known or that he'd squandered the last few years of their mother's tragically short life obsessively prospecting in Canada's kimberlite pipes for diamonds.

Sure, having the first diamond he'd found cut and set into a ring for her years after her death had certainly been a romantic gesture. But that hardly made up for the fact that he hadn't loved her enough to settle in one place when she'd been alive.

The one time he'd read the history of Messina Diamonds, all he'd seen were the stretched truths romanticizing a childhood that had barely been bearable for him.

But that wasn't what she'd seen. She'd seen exactly what the PR department had wanted her to see. Love, devotion and tragedy. A recipe for timeless romance.

And she'd fallen for it.

The ultimate proof that she wasn't nearly as practical as she wanted him to believe.

Though her ridiculous theories about his behavior certainly should have given him a clue what to expect. Apparently, she wanted to see him as some kind of wounded soul, tortured by his past. Her theory was damn near laughable.

But if he could use her sentimentality to get a yes out of her, then he would. If she was a closet romantic, he could give her romance. He could woo and seduce with the best of them. He certainly wasn't going to make the same mistake twice.

He felt only the briefest pang of concern for his motives, but he quickly buried it.

Isabella needed her mother. And since he wasn't willing to give up Isabella, marrying Lucy was the logical choice. After all the years he'd spent resenting his parents for the way they'd raised him, he took a certain amount of gratification in knowing that he would not make the same mistakes they had. He would put Isabella's needs and wants before his own. His proposal certainly was not the manifestation of some deeper desire to make Lucy his own. It was simply a matter of logic.

And next time, he wouldn't ask until he was sure of her answer. But eventually he would get a yes out of her. Because no wasn't an option.

Besides, if there was one lesson she should have learned by reading that garbage downstairs, it was that Messina men always got what they wanted.

"Don't look at me like that."

Lucy couldn't even meet Isabella's eyes as she ducked to pull her suitcase out from under the bed where she'd stashed it when she'd first arrived.

Isabella was currently having a little bit of "belly time" on her blanket in the middle of the king-sized bed. Her chubby little arms wobbled as she struggled to raise herself up enough to shoot Lucy what could only be described as an accusing glare.

"I'm not running away," Lucy continued in her own defense. "This is a strategic retreat, that's all." And really, she thought she'd shown quite a bit of fortitude in not retreating earlier. She'd allowed a whole nineteen hours to pass between Dex's proposal and her retreat. She hoisted the suitcase onto the foot of the bed and unzipped it. "I'm only leaving you with him temporarily."

But even as she said the words, she knew they were a lie. This wasn't temporary because chances were good she'd never get custody of Isabella. But if she was very lucky, and Dex was very forgiving, she'd at least get visitation rights.

She pulled a stack of clothes from the dresser drawer and tossed them into the suitcase. It seemed impossible that less than two weeks had passed since she'd first arrived at Dex's house. How had so much changed in so little time? How had she gone from mistrusting him to caring about him?

Moving about the room, she caught a glimpse of herself in the mirror over the dresser and stilled. Her eyes looked wide and haunted. Her cheeks sunken. Her skin pale. A sleepless night will do that, she told herself. Or maybe she'd had too much to drink last night.

But who was she kidding? Really?

She'd been lying to so many people lately, did she really need to start lying to herself as well?

This wasn't sleeplessness. This wasn't too much alcohol. She'd only had a single glass of champagne, for goodness' sake. This was good ol' fashioned misery. This was a broken heart.

Because she really had gone and done something stupid and fallen in love with Dex Messina.

What an idiot.

She'd fallen hard and fast for him. And she very much feared that her heart would be his forever. But that wasn't the reason—at least not the *only* reason—she was leaving now.

"Here's the plan, Isabella." She knelt down so she was eye to eye with the other person who owned a nice big chunk of her heart. "I'm going to tell him the truth."

Isabella parted her little rosebud lips.

"No, no." Lucy held up a hand as if staving off a protest. "Hear me out. He deserves to know. He deserves a chance to be a real father to you." She sucked in a deep breath. "And I'm going to track down your mother and sort this whole mess out. And in the meantime, I'm going to contact my lawyer and see if he can't arrange visitation rights."

Even though she should be packing, she couldn't resist picking up Isabella. She sat cross-legged on the bed and balanced Isabella on one knee.

"Don't you worry. He'll cave on visitation rights. I know he will. He's a stubborn man, but he's fair. He might be tempted to keep us apart just to punish me, but he'll do what's right for you."

Isabella frowned, giving Lucy the impression—not for the first time—that she really was listening. And while the practical side of Lucy knew she was mostly talking aloud for her own benefit, there was another side of her that truly believed Isabella understood—if not the words—at the least the emotions behind them.

"Here's the thing about dealing with your Dad. I know I warned you about letting him too close earlier. But I was wrong. Getting close to him is exactly what both of you need. Now, you may have to really work at this, because he's going to resist you every step of the way. But—" she met Isabella's gaze with a smile "—you have the advantage. You're cute and defenseless. You'll get him to open up. I've already seen you starting to work your magic on him. Besides, you worked your magic on me, didn't you?"

An instant later, her smile wavered.

Yes, Isabella had worked some pretty amazing magic on her.

Lucy hadn't needed anyone. And then Isabella had come

along, with her wide blue-gray eyes, her pink little mouth and soft fuzzy hair. One coo, one wobbly little smile and every defense Lucy'd had, had shattered.

Isabella had left Lucy's heart open and vulnerable.

And then Lucy had watched Isabella do the same thing all over again with Dex.

Lucy hadn't stood a chance. Dex didn't, either.

But now that she had to give Isabella up, Lucy didn't know how she was going to bear it. How could she possibly walk away from this sweet little girl?

Only one thing made it bearable. Knowing that Dex would be there to pick up where she'd left off.

"You're going to be just fine with him. You really are. He may not know it yet. But he loves you. And he's going to be a great father to you."

Lucy clutched Isabella to her chest. She squeezed her eyes closed, but couldn't keep the tears from seeping out of the corners of her eyes.

No, Isabella and Dex would both be fine. Lucy, on the other hand, felt like her very soul would be crushed by her sorrow.

By the time he found what he was looking for and made it back to the house, her bags were already packed and waiting by the front door.

Lucy stood in the entry hall, holding a sleeping Isabella in her arms, rocking slowly back and forth. Apparently waiting only to say goodbye to him before leaving.

"I won't let you take her."

Lucy looked up, frowning. "If I'd been planning on just taking her, I wouldn't still be here."

"Then what are you planning?"

"We need to talk." She gestured behind her and for the

first time he noticed the woman standing in the house, just beyond the foyer. "This is Mrs. Hill. She's a babysitter I've hired before. She's very reliable and Isabella knows her, so they'll be fine together."

"How long were you planning on talking?"

"I know I'm leaving you in a lurch, so tonight she's agreed to stay overnight with Isabella. She doesn't work weekends, but she's an experienced nanny. As long as you're home by seven most evenings, she can be here during the day while you're at work. I'm sure eventually you'll want to hire your own nanny, but until then—"

Tension knotted his belly as her words sank in. She was leaving.

Which, of course, the packed bags by the door indicated as well, but this was different. If she left and took Izzie with her, he had a built-in excuse for chasing her down. But if she left Isabella with him, that was something else entirely.

"I'm not going to hire a nanny. I want you to stay."

Exasperation crossed her face. "I can't stay indefinitely, Dex. You know that. You're going to have to hire a nanny eventually."

"I—"

But she raised a hand to cut him off. "We really do need to talk."

Wasn't this exactly the opportunity he'd been looking for? She wanted grand romance. Well, he was prepared to give it to her.

"In that case, we should go to the guesthouse where we can be alone."

With reluctance that was obvious even to him, she handed Isabella over to Mrs. Hill and followed him through the living room and kitchen out the back door and across the patio to the guesthouse.

The guesthouse was far more comfortable than the main house. Before moving into it six months ago, he'd had his own furniture moved in, so it reflected his more modern sensibilities.

When Lucy followed him in, her eyes scanned the room hungrily, taking in every detail.

"I wondered when I'd see it," she murmured.

"What?"

"Some scrap of your real personality."

A little fissure of irritation cracked through his grand plan to seduce her with romance. "It's just a room, don't make too much out of it."

He looked again. The leather sofa and armchair had clean, modern lines. The space was decorated in deep chocolate browns, smooth creams and cool, pale blues. It felt as much like home as anywhere he'd lived in the past decade. Which was to say, it was pleasant, but he was no more attached to it than to the hotel room he regularly stayed in at the Windsor Arms in Toronto.

"No, it's more than just a room. This is where you live." She swept the room with a gesture. "It suits you. It's restrained. Comfortable, but not fussy. I knew the big house—" she nodded in that direction "—wasn't you at all. It's too…"

When her words trailed off, he offered, "Garish."

Her lips twitched slightly. "I was going to say it's too comfortable with its wealth. You never seem at ease there."

He wasn't. But it annoyed him that she saw through him so completely.

"You're stalling," he pointed out. "There was something you wanted to talk about."

Instantly tension sprang into her body and he regretted changing the subject.

"I did." She turned away from him and paced to the far side of the room.

He watched as she put her purse down on the sofa and then picked it up again. Then put it down again. When she turned to face him again, her palm was pressed to her belly as if to quell her nerves.

"The thing is—" she broke off, sucked in a deep breath and started again. "Here's the thing. I'm not exactly who you think I am."

"I know."

Fourteen

"You do?" Her gaze darted to his.

He crossed to her side and took her shaking hands in his.

"You haven't hid it very well." Confusion lit her face. "Oh, you had me fooled at first. You seemed so practical. So down to earth. But that's not who you are. Not deep down inside."

Her frown deepened. "I don't know what you mean."

He brought his hand up to cup her face. The skin of her cheek was impossibly soft. Her lips were parted and dampened from her nervous licking. Her gaze softened. For a moment, the role he was playing faded into the background. The practiced seduction slid aside and in its place was some emotion he could barely name, let alone understand.

"You pretend to be so tough, but that's not who you are deep inside. You're a romantic. I didn't see that at first. But I do now."

She ripped her hands away from his, turning her face aside. "This isn't about me being a romantic."

"Of course it is. Last night when I proposed I did it all wrong. I didn't know you wanted a grand gesture."

She rolled her eyes. "Trust me. Unrolling about a million dollars worth of diamonds was grand enough. If I could have said yes, I'm sure I would have."

"Okay. The diamonds were grand, but they were impersonal. You wanted more." The role she needed him to play was coming more easily now.

When he handed her the wrapped package he'd taken out of storage earlier that afternoon, it almost felt natural.

"What is this?" she stared blankly at the gift-wrapped present.

"You wanted me to give you something personal. Unwrap it."

"Dex, I—"

But he cut off her protest. "This isn't easy for me. Just unwrap it, okay?"

Frowning, Lucy slipped her fingers under the edge of the wrapping paper and pealed it back to reveal a tattered, used copy of Mark Twain's *The Adventures of Tom Sawyer.*

This was no first edition family heirloom. No elegantly leather-bound copy. This was a cheap paperback. The cover creased, the pages yellowed and dog-eared and on the title page, stamped in faded blue print were the words, "Property of Spence Middle School."

She looked up at him as confusion replaced her distress. "I don't understand."

"I was in the seventh grade the year my mom was diagnosed with cancer. It was the only year we were in school the whole year. My English teacher read this book aloud."

His voice was oddly flat and emotionless as he spoke.

But as he had said, this wasn't easy on him. And she didn't need tears or outbursts of emotion to guess what this book had meant to him.

She could picture it all too well. The skinny, defensive adolescent boy, sitting in his English classroom, feeling so angry at the world—at his mother for being sick, at his father for not doing more—and slowly finding himself won over by the story of Tom Sawyer. The pranks, pratfalls and adventures would win the heart of any boy.

And then there was the fact that Tom was an orphan, drifting through life without need of parents or adults. How that must have appealed to Dex at a time when he'd felt his own parents had abandoned him.

Looking at the tattered old cover of Tom Sawyer, her heart seemed to swell and unfurl. Whatever few remaining defenses she had against this man crumbled and fell, leaving her completely vulnerable to him.

As she looked from the book to Dex she felt tears well in her eyes. "I…I don't know what to say."

"Say you'll marry me."

"I—"

"You wanted a romantic gesture." His mouth curved into a wry smile. "Personally, I thought the diamonds were much more romantic, but…"

He let his words trail off. He was waiting for her "yes."

She could feel it hanging there in the air between them. The expectation of acceptance.

He'd gone to all this trouble, searched his life—his whole history—for something personal enough to give her. Something "romantic" enough for her.

And she still couldn't say yes. He didn't know who she was. He would hate her when he did know.

Yet she found she couldn't say no, either. The word

seemed to have vanished from her vocabulary. Since she couldn't say yes and she didn't have the heart to tell him no, she did neither. Instead, she kissed him.

Sure, there were a thousand reasons why kissing him was just as stupid as saying yes. It was a momentary reprieve and nothing more. Yet she could think of nothing she wanted more at that moment than to press her body to his and pour into her kiss all the things she couldn't say. All the doubts and regrets. All the longing.

And she'd never get another chance. She'd have to come clean very soon, and the moment she did, he'd despise her. In all likelihood, this would be the last time he ever kissed her.

She had every intention of making the most of it.

His body was hard and solid beneath her hands. His muscles firm without being sculpted. His mouth was warm and bold against hers.

He accepted her kiss completely, without question. Maybe he thought it alone was the answer he sought. Whatever pang of conscious she felt at that, she quickly buried it. Maybe her acquiescence wasn't the answer he thought it was, but it was the answer of her heart.

When his hands sought the edge of her T-shirt and eased under the fabric to her bare skin, she didn't stop him. Instead, she relished the sensation of his roughened fingertips against the flesh of her stomach. His touch sent tendrils of desire pulsing through her.

Blood seemed to pound through her body, tightening her nipples, making the flesh between her legs throb. Her desire built all the more quickly because she knew what was coming. She knew what a powerful lover he was. How his touch would master her body. Make her tremble. How he would feel plunging into her, strong and hard.

She gasped aloud when his hand—finally—reached her breast. His touch was a little rough. Not painful, but firm. In control. Exactly what she wanted.

She didn't think twice before allowing him to nudge her legs apart with his knee. She welcomed the pressure against the apex of her legs and found herself bucking against him, aching for him to touch her there. To strip her jeans from her body, pull her panties down her legs and find the moistened folds of her flesh. To probe her body with his fingers, his mouth, and of course that glorious erection of his pressing against her hip.

She pulled her mouth from his, panting. "I want…"

But she trailed off, unsure how to put into words all she desired.

He looked down at her, his gaze clouded by desire, but a hint of amusement lingering on his lips as he toyed with her hardened nipple. "You want?"

"More," she gasped out. "I want you. All of you."

She'd never said truer words. It wasn't just his body she wanted thrusting against and into hers. She wanted his heart. She wanted him to give himself completely to her. Without reservations or doubts. She wanted to feel as if they were completely joined. Because when morning came and she had to tell him the truth, they would never be together again.

But she wouldn't let herself think of that for now. Now was just about them. About pleasure. About pouring her heart into every touch in hopes that someday he'd understand that she loved him despite the lies she'd told.

When he began backing her toward the bedroom, she let him. But she never released her hold on him. She clung to him as they moved through the living room, like a couple slow dancing to the rhythm of some sultry ballad. A kiss for every step. A tie loosened. A shirt pulled off. A snap undone. One shoe, then another kicked off.

By the time she felt his mattress bump against the back of her legs, she was down to just her jeans, unsnapped, unzipped, shoes off. His tie was gone, his white dress shirt unbuttoned. Still, she felt delightfully exposed by comparison. Wickedly naked.

He looked unbearably sexy, half-dressed as he was, the smooth muscles of his chest visible between the two halves of his shirt. The sprinkling of chest hair, the occasional glimpse of his nipples was enough to tempt her beyond endurance.

Pressing her hands against his shoulders, she spun him around so his back was to the bed. Then she shoved the shirt off his shoulders. It caught on his wrists, trapping his hands just long enough for her to give him one more light shove. He allowed himself to be toppled over, arms trapped at his sides, legs hanging over the sides of the bed.

She smiled in delight at the image he presented. He was completely at her mercy. And she intended to have none.

But first, she nudged her jeans down over her hips and let them fall to the floor. Any self-consciousness she might have felt standing nearly naked before him vanished at the sight of his appreciative smile curling his lips.

She supposed he could have been comparing her to the legions of women he'd no doubt been with before her, but the look in his eyes said he wasn't thinking of anyone else. Right now, at this moment, neither of their pasts existed. His other lovers didn't matter anymore than her lack of experience did.

All that mattered was tonight. This moment. This instant, as she was climbing on top of him, straddling his waist, staring down into the laughing eyes of the man whose body seemed to have been handcrafted for her pleasure.

She ran her hands over his chest, using his temporary confinement to explore his body and drive him crazy all at the same time. His skin was hot beneath her touch. His nipples were as hard as hers were and she took great pleasure in sucking each of them into her mouth, in the low moan of pleasure he gave as she raked them with her teeth.

"I think you're enjoying this," he ground out.

Leaning over his chest, up on her knees, she looked up at him. "I'd rather hoped you were, too."

He chuckled. "Oh, I am." Then his wicked smile vanished and his look intensified. "Don't forget. I'm not entirely without resources here."

His arms may have been trapped by his side, but his hands were still free and he was able to just reach the back of her knees. He grabbed her and with a swift tug, pulled her body up so that her mouth was even with his. He gave her a fast, fierce kiss.

"Unbutton my arms," he ordered.

"No."

Then, with another tug, he pulled her breasts within reach of his mouth. He laved first one breast and then the other with exquisite attention. His hands were at the back of her thighs now. She didn't know what was worse, the persistent sucking on her nipples or the aching anticipation of wondering how much range of motion he had in his arms.

Could his fingers reach her panties? Could they slip underneath?

His hands tightened on her thighs, branding her with his touch.

"Unbutton my arms."

"Make me." But the words came out as a pant. More begging than ordering.

Then with excruciating slowness, his hands moved from the backs of her thighs to the front. First one thumb and then the other slipped under the elastic edging of her panties. His thumbs moved to her entrance, where moisture clung. Moving in slowly expanding ovals, his thumbs circled from her entrance and then up, almost to her bud, and then back down.

With every movement, the tension seizing her body racketed up another notch. Almost there. Almost.

When his thumb finally brushed her center, her whole body clenched in a spasm, her back arching.

His hands tightened on her legs once more. This time, when he pulled her forward, she found herself poised directly over his mouth. His fingers tugged aside the only barrier separating them. He pulled her hips down and sucked her into his mouth. His tongue swirled around, his fingers slipped into her from behind and whatever remaining inhibitions she clung to vanished.

Suddenly, she was uncontrollable, bouncing on his fingers, moaning in pleasure, begging for more. Every muscle in her body tightened, poised for release. And then it came, as shock wave after shock wave of pleasure washed over her.

She was still trembling when he flipped her over onto her back. The last of their clothes vanished in the hazy aftermath of her climax. A second later his erection prodded her tender, sensitized fleshed, stirring her desire once more. He pounded into her, hard and fast. Touching the deepest part of her, pushing her to new heights of pleasure.

For an instant, her eyes drifted open, just long enough to see his expression, taut with desire, mindless with passion. And then she lost herself again as another climax shook her body and soul.

Fifteen

He still couldn't imagine how he'd possibly forgotten a sexual encounter with this woman. When he woke up the following morning to find her warm, naked body draped over his, he felt as if every instant of the previous evening had been branded into his mind.

The feel of her silken skin. The sight of her poised above him, head thrown back. The honeyed taste of her on his lips. The shuddering of her climax as her body had clenched around his.

She was, quite simply, unforgettable.

Every other woman he'd slept with faded into the recesses of his memory. All these years, he'd drifted from woman to woman, having one meaningless sexual encounter after another. He'd never before appreciated that knowing a woman would add so much to sex.

A glance at the clock told him it was far too early to wake

her. As appealing as early morning sex sounded, after the night they'd had, he wanted her to catch up on her sleep.

He slid out from under her, lingering only for a moment to brush the hair off her cheek. He didn't let himself stay longer. She was far too tempting as it was and he'd indulged his passions enough.

Last night's touching presentation of his old copy of *The Adventures of Tom Sawyer* had achieved his goal. She was going to marry him. She had, perhaps, not said the words, but her response hadn't left any room for doubt. Since he'd gotten what he'd wanted, he certainly didn't need to overplay his hand.

There'd been moments last night when he'd even felt himself swept up in his performance. Which, in the harsh light of morning, only reminded him that when they were married, he'd have to go the extra mile to make sure she didn't get too close.

He was his own man, in charge of his own destiny. He didn't need anyone. Not a seductive temptress like Lucy and certainly not a little imp of a baby girl. Trusting people, letting them close, meant heart-wrenching vulnerability. He'd learned that lesson long ago and it wasn't an experience he intended to repeat.

All the more reason—he thought as he pulled on a pair of jeans—not to linger in bed with her. Sex was one thing in a marriage. Explosive, amazing, best-sex-of-his-life sex—well, that was just a bonus. But he wasn't about to let himself be trapped by deeper emotions. He'd seen firsthand that love brought nothing to a marriage but heartache.

And he respected Lucy too much to break her heart.

He slipped into a pair of loafers and silently shut the bedroom door behind him before heading over to the main house.

It was only a little past six. The night before, Lucy had explained that she'd paid Mrs. Hill to stay the whole night. Originally, Lucy hadn't planned on being at the house much past their big "discussion." So Mrs. Hill had spent the night in the guest bedroom Lucy had stayed in previously, watching Izzie all through the night.

However, he knew Izzie sometimes woke up early. And since she'd been all night long without either parent, he'd like to be nearby when Mrs. Hill brought her down for her morning bottle.

Unfortunately, when he crept in through the back door, the house was silent and still. He quickly disarmed the alarm, then made his way over to the coffeemaker. While he waited for the machine to work its magic, he flipped absently through the pile of mail Derek's housekeeper had left at the kitchen desk the day before.

He shook his head in exasperation at the sight of a Pottery Barn Kids' catalog. How in the world had Pottery Barn found out he had a kid less than two weeks after he'd found out?

He tossed it aside along with the Hammacher Schlemmer catalog, quickly shuffled through a stack of bills and hesitated with the eleven-by-thirteen-inch envelope marked Confidential. The return address was Geneletic Labs. He stared at the envelope a moment before recognition sank in.

Geneletic Labs was the company he and Derek had sent their paternity test to the morning after Izzie had arrived on their doorstep.

Funny, when he'd taken the test just under two weeks ago, he'd been desperate to get the results. Desperate to know whether or not he could foist the responsibility for Izzie off on Derek.

He hadn't wanted her. Hadn't wanted to be tied down

by a child. Now, he knew there was nothing he wouldn't do for her. He'd even gladly made the sacrifice he'd once sworn he'd never make. He'd asked a woman to marry him. Hell, he'd damn near begged her.

Dex nearly tossed the unopened envelope into the pile of junk mail and catalogs. After all, he already knew he was Izzie's father.

But for some reason, he hesitated. With a why-the-hell-not shrug, he slipped his forefinger under the flap of the envelope and pried it open.

A moment later, he stared at the paper inside as shock rocketed through his body.

Isabella wasn't his.

So this, Lucy thought groggily, *was the meaning of the phrase "rude awakening."*

"Lucy, wake up," the stern voice repeated.

She rolled over onto her back, rubbing at her eyes and the words and the voice sank in.

That was Dex's voice. Dex, with whom she'd made beautiful, amazing love the night before.

Just as something warm and delicious began to unfurl within her, she was hit by another thought.

Dex, whose voice did not sound at all sleepy and sex-sated. Dex, to whom she still had not told the truth.

Dread quickly squashed any of her warmer emotions. Regardless of what had made him so grumpy this morning, the day couldn't end well. Not when she had such bad news to break to him.

Well, nothing like a cold dose of reality to wake one up, was there?

She sat up, pulling the sheet up to her shoulders as she did so. "What do you want?"

She tried not to sound defensive, but she wasn't at all sure she'd pulled it off. It would have been tricky, given his chilling scowl.

He stood at the foot of the bed dressed in jeans. Last night's dress shirt hung unbuttoned over his bare chest. His arms were crossed, his expression thunderous.

It was all she could do not to shrink into the bed and hide under the covers.

"Is Isabella okay?"

"Isabella is fine. At least, I assume she is." His scowl deepened. "She is not, however, mine."

Somehow his words just didn't register. "What are you talking about?"

"Isabella." He bit out the words. "She isn't mine."

"That's impossible." But even as she said the words, dread began to build in her stomach.

She looked up at him, but his expression—which was normally so cold—was thunderous.

"I don't understand."

He held up a sheaf of papers. "These are the test results from Isabella's paternity test. I'm not her father."

"But…I was so certain. I was so sure."

Her protests did little to soften his expression. He reached down, snatched up her shirt from the floor and tossed it on the bed. "Get dressed and get out of my bed."

Before she could respond, he stormed out, slamming the door to his bedroom. For a long minute, she just sat there in bed, staring at the yellow cotton T-shirt crumpled on the bed, her mind reeling and her stomach roiling.

How in the world had she made such a mess of things?

And could Dex really be right?

There was only one way to find out. She tugged the shirt over her head and stumbled from the bed. She found her jeans in a ball on the floor, but had to dig under the covers for her panties.

Her cheeks flushed as she pulled them on, unable to block the memories of the night before. The things she done with him…the things he'd made her feel…

And she had never even gotten to tell him the truth. Last night, in the heat of passion, she was sure she'd have plenty of time to explain first thing in the morning. Telling him the truth wouldn't have made her lies any easier to bear, but surely it would have made this situation a little better.

Before facing Dex, she snuck into the adjoining bathroom and splashed water on her face. She stared for a moment at her reflection. Her skin was pale and splotchy from shock. Her eyes red from lack of sleep. The short chunky haircut stood out in rumpled spikes.

Anxiety sat heavily upon her shoulders. Her emotions felt like they'd been cut out of her heart and trampled by a herd of elephants.

Turning her back on her reflection, she left the sanctuary of Dex's bedroom to face him. She found him in the living room of the guesthouse, with his forearm pressed against the window frame, staring out into the yard.

"Let me explain," she began.

But the look he shot her when he turned around sucked the words from her mouth. Oh, God. How could she explain this? Where could she begin?

"You don't need to explain. It's pretty obvious what happened."

"It is?"

"Obviously you had no idea who the father was. You just thought you could get the most money out of me."

"No. God, no. It was nothing like that. I thought she was yours. I swear I did. I didn't think she could be anyone else's."

"That's not precisely true is it?" He strode toward her, and without thinking she backed away from the threat. "'What if she's not yours?' Those were your exact words when you were trying to get me to give her back to you."

"I may have said that, but I didn't really believe it. I believed she was yours. I was just grasping at straws because I was desperate to get Isabella back. Even when I said it, I believed she was yours."

"But you knew it was a possibility that she wasn't."

"I—" She felt like she was drowning, struggling to resurface, to get on top of the conversation. But nothing she said would bring her head above water long enough for her to catch her breath. "I suppose I always knew it was a possibility that she wasn't yours. That there could have been someone else."

"Could have been?"

And then her mind, which had been desperately flailing about for something to latch on to, found the life preserver she'd been searching her. "But you said yourself she had to be yours. You said she had your father's eyes."

He let out a bitter, angry chuckle. "She does have my father's eyes. That's because Isabella is my brother's daughter."

Sixteen

"What?" Her question came out as a high-pitched squeak. "Your brother's? Are you serious?"

Dex's mouth was compressed into a thin, humorless line.

Well, apparently this wasn't his idea of a bad joke.

"Your brother? Your brother, Derek?"

In response, he merely handed her the papers he'd been holding.

It took her a long moment to read and make sense of what she was looking at. A detailed and rather extensive test to determine Isabella's paternity with two possible candidates, Dex and Derek. The letter briefly explained that because the two possible fathers were brothers, Isabella shared genetic markers with both of them. However, the test was conclusive. Derek was her father.

No, the joke was on her. And if anyone was laughing it was Jewel.

Jewel who, apparently, had slept with both Dex and Derek the month Isabella was conceived. It wasn't hard to piece together what happened. Jewel had had a crush on Derek. Despite Raina's insistence that he would never sleep with an employee, he obviously had slept with Jewel. When she'd been fired shortly thereafter, Jewel must have slept with Dex as revenge. Her way of proving to herself that Derek meant nothing to her. A few weeks later she'd found herself pregnant with no way of knowing which brother was the father.

Lucy's knees wobbled and gave out, forcing her to sink to the edge of the sofa as the enormity of the situation washed over her.

"I knew she'd slept with you." She was surprised to find herself speaking aloud. But what the hell. In for a penny, in for a pound. "I swear I had no idea she'd slept with anyone else. Let alone your brother."

For an instant, Dex's icy anger flickered with confusion. "What are you talking about?"

She sucked in a deep breath, pressed her hands to her knees and stood. That was the traditional way to face a firing squad, wasn't it?

"I know you're mad." He opened his mouth as if to cut her off, but she held up a hand to stop him. "Maybe even furious. But just let me explain."

"I think you'd better."

"I never slept with Derek."

He pointed to the sheaf of papers. "This rather expensive, scientific test says you did."

"*I* didn't sleep with him. *I'm* not Isabella's mother. I'm her aunt." A frown creased his forehead. Again, she held up her hands, though whether she did it to stave off his questions or as a sign of surrender, she wasn't sure. "My sister, Jewel, is her mother."

He gave a bark of bitter laughter. "I never slept with your sister."

She sighed, running her hand down her face. "She's my twin sister."

"Your twin?"

"Yes. My twin. The night you met my sister, Jewel, fifteen months ago, I was there at the bar. I knew she picked you up. I knew you slept with her. When she turned up pregnant a few months later, I just assumed you were the father."

"And decided to come looking for me?"

"No! It wasn't like that. You have to understand about Jewel. She means well, but she's flighty. Impatient. Impractical. But when she was pregnant with Isabella, she was different. For the first time in her life, she took something seriously. When she said she wanted to raise Isabella, that she was going to turn her life around, I believed her. Obviously, I encouraged her to contact you, to let you know you were going to be a father."

"Of course you did."

She ignored his comment and his sarcasm. It wasn't as if she'd done much to earn his trust. "But she refused. I can now see why. She said she wanted to do this on her own. And the first couple of months of Isabella's life, she did. But lately, she's been increasingly erratic. She and Isabella have lived with me since before Isabella was born. I love Isabella like she's my own daughter."

"Obviously."

"I'd even contacted a lawyer to get full custody of Isabella. And then one morning, I woke up and found them both gone."

"Two weeks ago."

She nodded. "I'm sure you can imagine how I felt. I wanted to believe she'd just gone out for the day, but the more I looked around the condo, the more worried I became. I couldn't tell if she'd taken any of her own clothes, but her makeup was gone. All her toiletries. When I realized Jewel had left Isabella at this house, I just assumed it was because you were the father."

She paused, sat down on the sofa again and rested her head in her hands. How could she explain? How could she possibly make him understand what her thought process had been like in those few panicky hours when she hadn't known whether or not Isabella was okay?

"You have to understand." She looked up at Dex, her expression pleading. "My first concern was for Isabella. I wanted to get her back. And I knew I could pass for Jewel if I changed my hair." She searched his face for any sign of softening. She saw none, so she stumbled ahead in her explanation. "I knew if I could just convince you that I was Jewel, that I was the woman you'd slept with, you'd believe I was Isabella's mother and you'd let me take her."

"And it never occurred to you that I might want to keep her? That I might care that I had a daughter?"

"I didn't know you then. I didn't know anything other than what I'd read in the papers. That you were the playboy rebel. Irresponsible."

His expression tightened, undoubtedly annoyed at the snap judgment she'd made about him.

She forced herself to her feet. If she was going to have to defend her decision, she was going to do it face-to-face. "I had no reason to assume you'd be a better parent than Jewel had. I knew her. She's my sister and I love her. But she abandoned Isabella. For all I knew, you wouldn't do better."

"Surely even I could do better than leaving a baby on the doorstep of a stranger."

His tone, heavy with sarcasm, only proved her arguments weren't swaying him. "Look." Her tone was sharp with anxiety and frustration. He wouldn't give her an inch. "You know how much I love Isabella. You know I'd do anything to protect her."

"Even sleep with me?"

His question hit her like a punch in the stomach. She reeled a step back, desperate for some space. "That's not how it was."

But he didn't let her retreat. He stalked closer, all his anger and frustration visible on his face. "Really? Then how was it? Why don't you explain to me exactly why you thought sleeping with me would help your cause? Did you think if you went to bed with me it would convince me you really were Isabella's mother?"

Her spine stiffened. "Now you're just lashing out. If you're only going to insult me, then there's no point in even discussing this."

She spun on her heel and headed for the door. She was several steps away when he grabbed her by the arm and spun her back to face him.

For just the briefest moment, the closeness of his body called to her. His expression, so tense, so unyielding reminded her of the previous night. Of the way he'd looked, poised above her as her body had writhed with passion.

How could that man—that man with whom she'd felt so close and free—be the same man fighting with her now? How could he accuse her of such awful things?

And why, dear God, hadn't she told him the truth earlier?

In that instant, she might have dropped to her knees and begged for forgiveness, but the moment was melodramatic enough without it.

That part of herself that wanted to supplicate to him evaporated with his next words.

"You're lucky I don't call the police and have you arrested."

For a moment she merely gaped at him, then she tugged her arm away from his. "You're right. I don't know why I did sleep with you."

For the first time that morning, something other than anger flickered across his face. But it was gone before she could even consider the possibility that she'd hurt him.

"Sleep with me? You were ready to marry me."

"I—"

"And how exactly did you think you were going to pull that off?"

"Don't be ridiculous. You know I was never going to marry you. I never said yes."

"Well, you didn't exactly say 'no,' did you?"

"I certainly did. And if you remember correctly, last night I told you we needed to talk. I was going to tell you the truth about Jewel. You're the one who stopped me. You're the one who wouldn't listen."

"And what exactly were you going to do after you'd told me?"

"I was going to leave. I'd realized that I was wrong about you. That you were going to be a good father. That you really did love Isabella."

"Of course I love her, I'm her father."

She knew the second Dex realized what he said was no longer true. A flash of pain so deep crossed his face there was no doubting it.

And that's when she knew she'd well and truly lost.

It didn't matter why she'd lied to him. She'd never convince him that her intentions justified her deception. In the end, he'd been too hurt by what she'd done. It wasn't about trust or deception anymore.

By pretending to be Jewel, she'd convinced him he was Isabella's father. In that short time he'd fallen in love with the girl he believed to be his. Her lie had ripped that dream away from him.

Nothing she could say or do would justify the pain she'd put him through.

All she could do now was step aside and let him mourn his loss. And pray that someday he'd at least understand what she'd done.

"She's not the mother."

Dex planted his hands in the center of Quinn's desk and leaned forward, so he was right in Quinn's face.

Quinn didn't flinch, but quirked an eyebrow. "Who isn't the mother?"

"Lucy. Lucy Alwin isn't Isabella's mother." Dex bit out the words, his rage emanating from every syllable. Overcome by the sudden urge to sweep all the papers off Quinn's desk, Dex forced himself to straighten and shoved his hands into his pockets. "You run a billion-dollar security business. You have legions of people at your disposal. Resources I'm sure I can't even imagine. Besides which, you're one of the smartest men I've ever known. So how the *hell* did one little woman—one actuary—manage to outsmart you?"

By now, Quinn's sardonic expression had faded to one of confusion. "What do you mean she's not Isabella's mother? If she isn't, then who is?"

"Her twin sister."

"Ah." Quinn rocked back in his chair. "That explains it. I would have needed her medical records to have found out. And you said you didn't want me to do anything illegal."

Dex turned away and paced to the far side of Quinn's

office, resisting the desire to yell at Quinn. This wasn't Quinn's fault. No, the only two people to blame here were Dex and Lucy. Which made it all that much harder to bear.

Quinn kept talking, apparently unaware of Dex's inner turmoil. "From a legal standpoint, this is good news. If both sisters were in on the deception, that should make it much easier for you to get custody of the girl."

"No, it won't. Isabella isn't mine."

"Oh."

That single word held a note of understanding that made the anger in Dex's stomach roil. The smug bastard thought he had it all figured out. Dex took little satisfaction in knowing that someday Quinn would meet a woman who would turn his life inside out.

"So that's what this is about," Quinn continued. "You've fallen for this kid and now that you've found out she isn't yours, you're understandably pissed off."

If only it were that simple. The problem was, this wasn't only about losing Isabella. It was also about losing Lucy.

Seventeen

There were times—and this was one of them—when he wondered why he even came in to work. Since this was corporate headquarters, Derek all but insisted at least one of them be there at all times. Yet the reality was, Derek did his job so well from no matter where he was, that Dex often contributed very little to this company in comparison to his brother's endeavors.

Which left Dex way too much time to consider the many years he had ahead of him of having not much to do.

Still, when he heard the door to his office open he didn't appreciate the interruption. Quinn was the only one who would just let himself into his office. And Quinn really should have known better.

"Damn it, Quinn—" But he broke off when he saw not Quinn, but Lucy enter the room.

"Don't blame him. He was going to have me arrested. Or

at least thrown out. But I bullied him mercilessly to convince him to let me up. I pulled out all the stops. Even tears."

As evidence, she held out one of the crisp white handkerchiefs Quinn always kept tucked in his suit pocket.

Dex felt his jaw clench. Despite himself, he couldn't help noticing how good she looked. Which was ridiculous, since she looked horrible. Splotchy complexion, red nose, dark circles under her eyes. And she'd pulled her hair into a stubby ponytail rather than her normal sassy bob.

He should be rejoicing. After all, if things had been different, they'd be engaged right now and soon he'd be trapped in a marriage to a liar. So why did he instead want to cross the room and pull her into his arms?

Somehow, his subconscious must not accept what his conscious mind knew to be true: this woman meant nothing to him.

"Looks like I'll have to review security procedures with Quinn. In the meantime, if he's feeling too sentimental to have you thrown out, I'm sure I can find someone else who isn't." He made to reach for the phone, though he knew he'd never follow through.

Before his hand even touched the handset, Lucy rushed across the room and stopped him by putting her hand on his.

"I only need a few minutes." She held up a duffel bag he hadn't noticed before now. "I just stopped by to drop off this bag of Isabella's clothes. At least…" she hesitated. "At least, that's ostensibly my reason for stopping by."

"What is it you want, Lucy?" Her name came out with a little bit of bite to it. Even speaking her name was a reminder of the lies she'd told.

"To apologize. I'm not very good at owning up to my mistakes. It's just that I…I don't like making them. I've spent all my life trying to be the perfect daughter. The perfect student. The perfect employee. I don't like failing."

She paused to suck in a deep breath, and despite himself, he found his defenses against her weakening.

"Which only makes it harder when you have to admit to making a huge, colossal mistake like the one I made. I know what I did really messed up your life for a few weeks. But you have to know, I really did believe I was doing the right thing for Isabella. I just got so centered on what I thought was right for her, I didn't think about what was right for anybody else."

She flashed him a game little smile, like she'd made a bad joke but wanted him to laugh at it anyway. He didn't. He couldn't laugh at anything, not even bad jokes.

Her eyes narrowed as she looked at him, giving him the impression she was assessing his very soul. And probably finding it lacking.

"You know, Dex, this act may work with other people, but I don't buy it."

"This act?" he asked sardonically.

"You, sitting there behind the desk, so cool. Obviously you want me to believe that all of this means nothing to you. That you haven't been affected by any of this. But I know the truth. I've seen how you are—how you were—with Isabella. You really love her. And it's got to be killing you that she's not your daughter."

Having her here was bad enough. Listening to all this crap about his emotions was more than any man should have to up with. "What exactly is it you want from me, Lucy? If you're expecting some sappy outpouring of emotion, I'm afraid you've come to the wrong man."

"Yes. I suppose I have." Her expression tightened as grim lines settled around her mouth. "Thank goodness I didn't expect that. I guess I just wanted to admit that I was wrong. And to apologize and—"

"And you expect me to forgive you?" A note of bitterness crept into his voice. As much as he hated how weak it made him sound, he kept talking. "You expect me to offer you absolution? Or assuage your guilt?"

"No. Trust me. I'd never expect that. You're not a very forgiving man, Dex. You still haven't forgiven your parents for dragging you around the world when you were kid. Or your brother for not being there when you needed him. I certainly don't expect you to forgive me for this.

"What I want is to make sure Isabella isn't going to pay the price for my mistake." She paused as if waiting for him to say something. When he didn't respond, she sent him a searching look and seemed to find him lacking. She just shook her head. "I bet you haven't even seen Isabella since you found out she's not yours. I bet you can't even look at her."

"Mrs. Hill is with her. If you're implying she isn't getting competent care—"

"Mrs. Hill is more than competent. But Isabella needs people near her who love her. If I can't be there, then she needs her uncle."

He planted his hands on the desk in front of him. "So this is really just another bid to get custody of her?"

If he expected a burst of anger, he was disappointed. She merely shook her head as if disillusioned with him. "You should know me better than that. This isn't about what I want. It's about what's best for Isabella. I don't know your brother. He knows how to run a company, but is he going to be a good father?"

She rounded his desk, got right in his face and stared up at him, her expression pleading.

"I'm not willing to leave it up to chance. I'm going to fight for her." He opened his mouth to protest, but she put her hand on his face, shushing him with her gentle touch. "This can't be a surprise to you. You had to know I'd do this. I'm going to see my lawyer this afternoon. I'm not asking for full custody. I don't think there's a court in the country that would give me that. Just partial custody. But if I don't get it, then it's going to be up to you to make sure your brother has what it takes to be the kind of dad she needs.

"Derek may be a great CEO," she continued. "But he'll probably need help from you to become a great dad. You can't let your past differences get in the way."

"Trust me, Lucy. You're the worst person to be giving me advice about how to live my life."

"No. I'm the best person. I know better than anyone else that you're hardest on the people closest to you. The more you care about them, the less likely you are to forgive them for making mistakes. For being human. But Dex, if you can't forgive other people's mistakes, how are you ever going to forgive your own mistakes? And trust me, this mistake you're about to make—of pushing Isabella out of your life— It's a real doozy. If you don't make the effort to work things out with your brother and then Isabella ends up paying the price, you'll never forgive yourself. I don't want you to have to go through that. I love you too much."

He scoffed. "A bit melodramatic, don't you think?"

She smiled a wry, sad little smile. "You know me, I'm the romantic one." She turned to leave, but stopped just before she reached the door. "Just out of curiosity, *Tom Sawyer?*"

His blank expression was all the answer she needed.

She nodded. "That's what I thought. Just a ruse, huh?"

"You wanted a big romantic gesture."

"Where did you get the copy of the book?"

"I had a couple of boxes in storage. Just stuff from when I was a kid."

"I bet you've never even read it, have you?"

"If I did, I don't remember. How did you guess?"

"Just a hunch." She was hurt but not surprised by his admission. Their whole relationship had been built on lies. Maybe she should be reassured that she wasn't the only one telling them.

Just before closing the door behind her, she looked over her shoulder and said, "You should try reading it sometime. It's a good book. You might find it brings back more of your childhood than you think it will."

He appraised her coolly. "I'm hardly the type to try to reclaim my childhood innocence."

"No. But maybe you should be."

He didn't go looking for *Tom Sawyer*. In fact, if he ever happened upon the damn thing, he'd resolved to toss it in the trash. Burning it held a certain appeal but seemed to give the book more significance than it warranted.

It was pure bad luck then that the same day Lucy had come to his office happened to be the same day Mavis cleaned the guesthouse, top to bottom, during which she must have found the tattered old copy of *Tom Sawyer*, so that when Dex arrived home at just after nine, the first thing he saw was the book, sitting in the middle of the kitchen counter.

The sight of the book stopped him in his tracks, just inside the door. He stared at it as emotions rushed through him. Finally, he swooped across the room, snatched the book from where it sat on the counter and carried it straight to the trash can. He stomped on the trash can's foot pedal and the lid sprang up. He stood there for a long moment, holding the book poised over the fresh white trash bag.

"Damn it," he cursed softly, dropping the book into the otherwise empty trash can. He moved his foot, letting the lid snap closed with a clang of finality.

Then, with forced calm, he grabbed a Shiner out of the fridge, twisted the cap off and didn't even look at the book when he dropped the bottle cap in the trash can. Taking a gulp of beer, he loosened his tie and pulled it off. In the bedroom, he avoided looking at the bed, as he had ever since the night he'd shared it with Lucy.

If Mavis—who came by the guesthouse every day to make the bed and pick up—had noticed that he'd spent the past three nights sleeping on the sofa in front of the TV, she wisely hadn't said anything.

Dex changed into jeans, leaving on his dress shirt but not bothering to tuck it in. Then, with pointed determination, he sat himself down in front of the TV, as he had the past three nights, and grabbed the remote. He scanned through all three-hundred-and-sixty-four channels. Twice.

Before he could make a third round, he happened to glance out the window toward the main house. Lights were on in both the kitchen and the living room. Through the uncurtained window, he caught a glimpse of a form pacing back and forth. Mrs. Hill, he realized, walking with Izzie.

"Isabella, damn it." He sat up, thumped his beer bottle on the table before him and dropped his head into his hands.

She wasn't his. Izzie was the cute nickname a doting father bestowed on his daughter. But he wasn't a father.

Three days he'd known it, and the loss and resentment still burned in his gut. Still kept him up at nights. Which was ridiculous. He'd never wanted to be a father. Hadn't ever wanted a tiny baby girl with copper curls and his father's eyes. Hadn't ever dreamed there'd be a woman he desired so strongly he couldn't even sleep in the bed in which he'd made love to her.

He sure as hell hadn't known that losing them both would be like having his heart ripped out. But they weren't his to keep. They weren't his family.

But—he straightened slowly as the realization hit him—Isabella didn't know that. She didn't know the difference between a mother and an aunt. Between a father and an uncle.

All she knew was that the two people who'd cared for her most were suddenly gone.

No matter how competent Mrs. Hill was, she couldn't make up for the lost love of an aunt or an uncle.

Only a few minutes had passed by the time he made it down the guesthouse stairs and across the yard to the kitchen door.

Mrs. Hill—who had been pacing around the kitchen island, Isabella clutched in her arms—looked up when he entered, a harried expression on her face. Isabella wailed in indignation.

"I'm sorry, Mr. Messina," she blurted out. "I didn't realize you could hear her crying from over in the guest-house. I can take her back up—"

"No." He interrupted her. "She didn't bother me. How long has she been crying?"

"A couple of hours. It's nothing to worry about," she hastily reassured him. "Babies just need to cry it out some-times. It's just colic, nothing serious."

Mrs. Hill's words barely registered. His attention was so completely focused on Isabella, he hardly knew Mrs. Hill was there.

It had been days since he'd seen her. Since the morning he'd found out she wasn't his. The morning he'd hired Mrs. Hill to watch her twenty-four hours a day until Derek got back. And then, he'd barely let himself look at her.

Tonight, her tiny face was flushed red from exertion. Tears and snot ran down her cheeks and chin. She'd never looked more beautiful to him.

He crossed to Mrs. Hill and held out his hands. "You could probably use a break."

Mrs. Hill hesitated. "You're not paying me to take breaks. I can handle her."

"I know you can. But it's been pointed out to me lately that I haven't been a very good uncle."

"Nonsense!" Mrs. Hill protested, but she let Dex slip his hands under Isabella's tiny arms and take her into his arms.

Isabella protested by ratcheting her cries up a notch.

"Oh, dear," Mrs. Hill reached for her, but Dex stepped out of her reach.

"We'll be okay. You said yourself there wasn't anything wrong with her. Why don't you go get some rest? I'll come get you if we need anything."

Mrs. Hill twisted her hands together. "Well, if you're sure…" She stood in the doorway a long time before slowly backing away. "She ate about an hour ago so…"

"I'll give her another bottle in an hour or two. Thanks."

As Mrs. Hill disappeared around the corner, he settled Isabella more closely to his chest. He felt her body, warm and fragile in his arms, her tiny hands pushing against him in protest, her cries—quieter now—slowed and softened. The weight of her against his chest seemed to melt something deep inside of him. He felt as though his chest had opened up and she'd slipped right inside of his heart. Like her body had melted into his, become a physical part of him that he'd be unable to function without.

He'd felt that same way the first time he'd fed her and

felt her fall asleep in his arms. That first time he'd acknowledged that he was her father.

The sensation—the emotions—were no different for knowing that he wasn't her father. To him, father or uncle felt exactly the same.

He'd still do anything to protect her. Anything to keep her safe and let her know she was loved. To his heart, it didn't matter one bit that she wasn't actually his daughter.

Automatically, he slipped into the slow, rhythmic waltz that had calmed her previously. As her cries slowed and she nuzzled his chest with her tear-dampened face, a realization rocked through him.

This must be how Lucy felt about her.

It didn't matter that she wasn't her mother. The love and devotion was there, regardless. It hardly mattered who her parents actually where.

Isabella stared up at him from under her tear-spiked lashes. And as he stared back into her blue-gray eyes, he knew just how Lucy felt. He'd do anything to protect this child. Lying? Yep. Even to someone he cared about, if he thought Isabella's health and happiness were at stake.

And then it hit him. The real reason he hadn't yet told Derek he was a father. Dex hadn't decided completely that he *was* going to tell him.

He had to tell Derek, of course, but until he did, the possibility of not doing so still lingered in the back of his mind.

But Lucy was certainly right. Derek wasn't prepared for this. Dex would have to work hard to whip his brother into fatherly shape.

"Don't worry," he murmured to Izzie. "I won't let him screw up too badly."

In response, Izzie merely snuffled and stared up at him. She blinked slowly and he saw a question in her eyes.

"What do you mean, 'What about Lucy?'"

Isabella blinked again, the last of her cries dying out.

"You don't expect me to just forgive her, do you?"

If he didn't know better, he'd have sworn she rolled her eyes at him.

He flicked off the lights in the kitchen and waltzed his way toward the back door as he felt her beginning to relax against him.

Despite his teasing tone with Izzie, Lucy's betrayal still sat heavily on him. But what had she done that he wouldn't have?

She had put Izzie's needs before everything else. Before her own needs. Before his.

All his life he'd resented the fact that his parents hadn't done the same. Could he really blame Lucy for acting exactly in the manner he'd want the mother of his children to act?

As he let himself into the guesthouse, he felt Izzie sigh against his chest, her breath warm and moist at the open collar of his shirt.

"Yeah. I guess you're right."

He crossed to the trash can, popped open the lid and stared at the copy of *Tom Sawyer* lonely in the bottom of the can. He reached in, flicked the bottle cap aside, and pulled the book out.

Eighteen

She'd been summoned to Messina Diamonds. Via her lawyer, no less.

If Dex Messina wants to talk to you without lawyers present, it would be wise to attend, her own lawyer had said. *Down the road, if this case goes to trial, you want it to look like you did everything in your power to settle this amicably.*

As she circled the block for the third time looking for a parking spot, Lucy contemplated what an odd word choice that was. *Amicably.* In the spirit of friendliness.

But things between her and Dex had never been friendly. Tender, passionate, fraught with emotion, yes. Friendly? No.

And at this point, she couldn't imagine anything either of them could say or do that would change things between them.

It all came down to this. She'd lied to him and deceived him. And he'd never be able to forgive her for that. It didn't seem to matter to him that she'd fallen in love with him in the process. Or that he'd lied to her as well, in his own way.

They'd both made mistakes, she rationalized as she rode in the elevator. Too bad she was the only one interested in overcoming their differences. That—she supposed—was what she got for falling in love with such a stubborn man.

At least she could face him having finally talked to Jewel. After all this time, Jewel had returned Lucy's phone calls. It turned out that Isabella's conception had occurred much as Lucy had imagined it. After sleeping with Derek and being fired by him, she'd set out to seduce Dex on a vengeful whim. She'd let Lucy believe he was the father all those months because it was easier than explaining the truth. Just as dumping Isabella on Derek and Dex's doorstep had been easier than facing either man.

On Jewel's part, there had been many tears and a lot of posturing, but she'd never acknowledged that abandoning Isabella was wrong. Lucy had ended the conversation more frustrated with her sister than ever. She could only hope that her impending conversation with Dex would go better.

Within mere minutes of walking into the building, she was being shown into Dex's office. It was empty when the secretary left Lucy alone in it. She stood in the middle of the room for a moment, feeling awkward before propping her hands on her hips and glaring at the empty room.

"Typical," she muttered aloud before crossing to his desk and nosing around unrepentantly.

She stared down at the meticulously organized desk, looking for some clue as to why he'd asked her here today. A laptop sat on one wing of the desk at a ninety-degree angle from an empty in-box. On the corner of the otherwise blank blotter sat a small familiar jewelry box. It looked lonely there on the desk. As if Dex had set it there the evening she'd returned the ring to him.

"Typical," she muttered a second time. Apparently Dex had just left the ring in his office all this time, not even bothering to put it someplace safe.

By the time she heard the door open and close behind her, she was feeling even more disgruntled than she had when she'd first received his summons.

She turned to face him, but her words got momentarily caught in her throat at the sight of him.

"You don't look happy to be here," he observed.

As always, he was dressed impeccably in a navy suit. The crisp white of his dress shirt accented his tan. However, his eyes were lined with exhaustion and his hair looked as if he'd been running his hands through it.

She felt a pang of sympathy for him before repressing the urge to cross the room and rub the tension from his shoulders. Yeah, he'd certainly appreciate that, wouldn't he?

"How should I look? There's not much to be happy about in this situation."

"No. I don't suppose there is."

"And frankly, I can't even imagine why you'd want to see me again. The last time I was here was hardly a successful meeting."

He ignored her comment as if she hadn't even spoken. Which was a bit disappointing, because she was really curious why he'd wanted to see her.

"I received a letter from your lawyer the other day."

"That can't be unexpected. I told you I would try to get partial custody of Isabella."

And she refused to feel the least bit guilty for it, either.

He crossed to his desk and pulled a single sheet of paper from the drawer.

"What surprised me was that it came to me. Instead of Derek."

"Oh." She hadn't even considered to whom her lawyer would send the letter. It hadn't occurred to her to ask.

"Did you think I'd be more sympathetic to your cause?"

"I wouldn't dream of presuming that."

"But—" Again he continued as if she hadn't spoken, though his voice had softened a bit. "I suppose I am."

She blinked in surprise but could think of no response.

"I've given it a great deal of thought. Once Derek finds out Isabella is his and once he learns about your role in all of this, he's unlikely to so much as give you a chance to explain, let alone to be a part of Isabella's life. I may be unforgiving, but Derek is the control junkie in the family. He'll approach raising Isabella like a business venture and he'll see you as a rival. He'll do everything in his considerable power to guarantee you never even see her again."

Listening to Dex's description of Derek, Lucy felt her knees wobble, forcing her to drop to the chair opposite Dex's desk.

"I hope this isn't your idea of a pep talk."

Of course, he hadn't told her anything she didn't already know. Yet somehow hearing him say it made the threat seem all the more real.

"The way I see it, you have only one option." He rounded the desk and came to stand in front of her, hip propped on the edge of his desk, long legs stretched out in front of him.

Once again his sexual charisma slammed into her. Reminding her that more than her relationship with her niece was at stake here. Her heart was in danger, as well.

Though in danger of what, she couldn't really say. He'd already broken her heart, rejected her when she was at her most vulnerable. What more damage could he do?

Bolstered by that thought, she stood, crossed her arms over her chest and faced him head-on. "And what option is that?"

"Marry me."

She laughed outright. A sharp bark of laughter full of incredulity, but not humor. "You're asking me to marry you? Again?"

"Yes."

"What, third time's the charm? You can't be serious."

"I am." He propelled himself away from the desk and took a single step, closing the distance between them. "The third time will be the charm, only if I can do it right this time. Marry me, Lucy. Not because it's the right thing for Isabella but because it's the right thing for me."

The intensity of his expression made her breath catch in her chest. Still, she forced herself to be rational. Not to be manipulated by those romantic tendencies he was all too capable of using against her.

"You mean it's the easy thing for you," she pointed out.

This time, he was the one who laughed. But instead of cynicism, there was genuine warmth in his laughter. "Lucy, when have you ever been easy on me?"

"Good point."

He reached up to cradle her face in his hands. "You drive me crazy. You make me doubt myself and question everything I do. Being married to you definitely won't be easy. But I need you."

Her heart felt tight in her chest. She so desperately wanted to believe him. But she'd been fooled by him before. Been tricked into believing in sincerity when sincerity wasn't there.

"Let me guess. You need someone to pick up your laundry and you think I'll fall for it since you can dangle Isabella in front of me like a carrot."

"No. I need you, Lucy. Not someone else. Just you. You're the only one capable of breaking down these walls I've been building around myself. You're the only one who can teach me how to be an uncle and a husband and a father. You're the only one I want to bear the child I didn't even know I wanted to have. It's got to be you, Lucy. You're the only one up to it."

"Children?" she asked, more than a little in shock.

"You didn't think after teaching me to be a dad I'd be willing to settle for being just an uncle, did you? Besides, Isabella needs cousins."

"Dex, how can you ask me to marry you when you haven't even forgiven me for lying to you about who I was?"

"Who says I haven't forgiven you?"

"Well…" She fumbled for a moment, searching for an answer. "Logic does. I can barely forgive myself for the way I messed up your life, for how my lies hurt you. I thought I was doing the right thing for Isabella, but—"

"Exactly. You were doing what you thought was right for Isabella." He took her hands in his, his thumbs tracing delicate circles around their backs. "All my life I've blamed my parents for not putting our needs before their own. How can I blame you for doing the opposite? Every decision you made, you thought of her first. That's exactly what I'd want from the mother of my children."

"I…I don't know what to say."

"Say 'yes.'" And then his lips quirked into a smile. "A definite yes would be nice this time."

And, oh, dear God, she wanted to. Pure yearning nearly pulled out of her the "yes" he wanted. Only caution held her tongue.

She had to force herself to step away from him. "It's not that I don't want to say 'yes'—"

"Then what is it? Another secret identity you've kept hidden from me? Another child of your sister's you've been pretending was your own?"

Because there was still humor in his voice, she forced herself to smile. But before she could voice her protest, he grabbed the ring box and went down on one knee. Popping the box open with his thumb, he presented it to her.

Nestled within the black velvet of the jeweler's box was a ring, but not the one she'd expected. Set into a simple platinum band was a round, blue-green stone, its surface polished smooth to reveal a pale six-rayed star.

She looked from him to the ring and back. "It's lovely. Is it an opal?"

"No, it's a star sapphire."

"Oh." She wasn't sure what he expected her to say.

"You want to know the real reason I never gave you that damn ring from my father? I don't like diamonds."

"Oh," she repeated, this time with dawning comprehension, as a glimmer of hope pierced her confusion.

"Actually, I hate the things. That particular one more than most. To me, it doesn't represent love, it's just proof of his stubborn tenacity."

"Then why—"

"Why did I give it to Isabella? Because whether or not I like them, isn't the point. That ring is part of her heritage. I may not want it, but someday she probably will. Of course, I could give you some other diamond. But I don't like any of them. I think they're plain and colorless. They're boring. They're not even particularly rare. People only value them because advertising companies have worked hard to make them the symbol of everlasting love."

He stood, took the ring box from her fingers and pulled the ring out. Taking her hand in his, he slid the ring onto her ring figure. "But look at the star sapphire. Look at its brilliant color. Look at the way it moves in the light." He gently twisted her wrist first in one direction, then the other. As he did so, the star seemed to shimmer across the surface of the stone. "It's almost alive. It's enchanting. It's a stone you could look at every day for the rest of your life."

A faint gasp escaped her lips as she twisted her hand, watching the star's progression across the stone.

"Of course, I could just grab a big diamond from the family vault if you'd prefer." He made to remove the ring from her finger.

She jerked her hand away, with a giggle. "No. It's mine now. You're not getting it back that easily."

"But you're still hesitating."

And how could she explain that after he'd gone to such lengths to give her the big gesture, she wanted the little words to go with it. That without them, she couldn't really *believe*.

"I'm just afraid…" She stepped away from him, giving herself a little room. "Look, the woman you think you want doesn't even exist. You were never really attracted to me. You wanted my sister, or rather, what you remembered of her. Some exotic stranger you met in a bar. That was the woman you desired."

He actually had the gall to laugh at her. She felt a stab of pain, deep in her heart. Just when she thought her defenses against him would hold…

"How shallow do you think I am? No, wait. Don't answer that. I already know." He took her chin in his hand and forced her to look up at him. "I'm not some high school boy to be manipulated. I know what I want. And don't flatter yourself. You're not that good of an actress."

Before she could protest, he continued on.

"You never really pulled off pretending to be your sister.

I never mistook you for some good-time party girl I'd picked up in a bar. I never thought you were just some 'exotic stranger'—to use your term. I always knew you weren't the woman I picked up at the bar that night."

"How? What do you—"

"Oh, I believed you were Isabella's mother alright. I believed you were physically the woman I'd slept with. But I knew you were different. I just assumed motherhood had changed you. Transformed you into someone I could imagine loving. You said I'd fallen in love with an illusion."

"I never claimed you'd fallen in love," she protested.

"Ah." Awareness flickered across his face. "No, you didn't, did you? You accused me of feeling attraction. Not love. I bet you still don't even believe I love you."

"I—"

He tilted her chin up to face him more fully, but she refused to meet his gaze.

"The truth is, I barely remember meeting and sleeping with your sister. If you hadn't shown up on my doorstep, I literally never would have given her a second thought. It's you I can't get out of my head. It's you I love."

Once again he cradled her face in his palms. This time, he leaned down to press a kiss to her lips. Unlike every other kiss they'd shared, this one was gentle. A delicate request. Light as air and soft as the morning sun drifting through a window.

When he pulled back, his heart and his love were in his eyes. "Don't make me ask you a fourth time because you know I'm not going to give up this easily."

"Yes." And she kissed him again. "Yes, Dex. I'll marry you."

As he kissed her again—a real Dex kiss this time—she couldn't help but marvel at her luck. All she'd done in the past month was make mistakes. And somehow it had still ended perfectly.

Epilogue

Isabella, now a rambunctious fourteen-month-old, sat in her high chair, swinging her legs back and forth, kicking the base of the table. One hand clutched the handle of a sippy cup, the other a fistful of Cheerios.

Dex shot an exasperated look at Lucy. "I don't think she understands."

Lucy, suppressing a smile, crossed to where he sat in the chair beside Isabella's high chair. She rubbed her hand along his shoulder, soothing the lines of tension in his muscles. He shifted toward her and she automatically stepped between his open legs. "Of course she doesn't understand. Not really."

Dex tugged on her arm, pulling her down onto his knee. She wrapped an arm around his shoulder and leaned into his chest, marveling at his strength. Relishing the feel of his body against hers, so strong and comforting.

Marveling at her luck, as well. This man would do anything for her. Anything for the child she now carried in her belly.

Dex absently ran a hand over her protruding stomach, obviously not even noticing that the muscles were taut with a contraction of early labor. To Isabella, he said, "The new baby will take a lot of our attention at first. But that doesn't mean we love you any less."

Isabella giggled, no doubt amused by her uncle's serious expression and tone. She brought her fist to her mouth and shoveled in the Os. With one still clinging to her lips, she brought the tips of her fingers together in the baby sign for "more."

Lucy put another handful of Cheerios on the tray of Isabella's high chair, her heart so full she thought it might burst. She had more joy in her life than she'd ever imagined. A child on the way. A husband who loved her. A niece she adored and—now that Lucy and Dex had moved into their own house—who lived just around the corner.

She and Dex might not be Isabella's parents, but they were still very much a part of her life. Frankly, Lucy couldn't ask for more.

"You're allowed to be a little jealous of the new baby," Dex was saying to Isabella. "But just remember, he's going to be your cousin. It'll be your job to show him the ropes. And keep him in line. Just don't be too much of a bully."

Not wanting Dex to see how cute she thought his concern was, Lucy turned her face into his neck so he wouldn't see her smile.

A moment later the doorbell rang.

"I wonder who that is."

"It's Mrs. Hill," Lucy told him as she stood. "I—"

"Why is she here?"

"Well, we need someone to watch Isabella," she pointed out gently. "We—"

"I hope you're not planning on going somewhere. Do you have any idea how long it took me to convince Derek to let us have Izzie for the whole evening?"

After a very rocky start, Derek had eventually taken to fatherhood, approaching it with the same steel-jawed determination with which he approached everything. It was more than a little amusing to watch. However, at the moment, she had more pressing matters on her mind.

Lucy exhaled slowly as the contraction faded and the muscles of her belly began to relax. "Remember, we talked about giving birth at home, but the last time I checked you were adamantly opposed." She paused, waiting for comprehension to dawn on Dex's face. When he still looked confused, she continued. "Since I'm pretty sure I'm in labor right now, we probably want to head to the hospital."

"You're in labor?" Dex's face went white.

"Yep."

"Right now?"

She nodded. "It's still early, but you've been so worried about getting to the hospital…"

He stood so quickly he knocked the chair over. Isabella let out a delighted peal of laughter. Lucy held back her own chuckle as she watched a mixture of anxiety, excitement and wonder drift across Dex's face.

They'd already shared so much together and still had so much more to experience. They had a whole lifetime to look forward to. And Lucy planned on enjoying every minute of it.

* * * * *

Don't miss Derek's story, part of the
BILLIONAIRES & BABIES *series,*
available from Silhouette Desire,
October 2008.

*Look for LAST WOLF WATCHING
by Rhyannon Byrd—the exciting conclusion
in the BLOODRUNNERS miniseries
from Silhouette Nocturne.*

*Follow Michaela and Brody on their fierce journey
to find the truth and face the demons from the past,
as they reach the heart of the battle between
the Runners and the rogues.*

*Here is a sneak preview of book three,
LAST WOLF WATCHING.*

Michaela squinted, struggling to see through the impenetrable darkness. Everyone looked toward the Elders, but she knew Brody Carter still watched her. Michaela could feel the power of his gaze. Its heat. Its strength. And something that felt strangely like anger, though he had no reason to have any emotion toward her. Strangers from different worlds, brought together beneath the heavy silver moon on a night made for hell itself. That was their only connection.

The second she finished that thought, she knew it was a lie. But she couldn't deal with it now. Not tonight. Not when her whole world balanced on the edge of destruction.

Willing her backbone to keep her upright, Michaela Doucet focused on the towering blaze of a roaring bonfire that rose from the far side of the clearing, its orange flames burning with maniacal zeal against the inky black curtain of the night. Many of the Lycans had already shifted into their preternatural shapes, their fur-covered bodies standing like monstrous shadows at the edges of the forest as they waited with restless expectancy for her brother.

Her nineteen-year-old brother, Max, had been attacked by a rogue werewolf—a Lycan who preyed upon humans for food. Max had been bitten in the attack, which meant he was no longer human, but a breed of creature that existed between the two worlds of man and beast, much like the Bloodrunners themselves.

The Elders parted, and two hulking shapes emerged from the trees. In their wolf forms, the Lycans stood over seven feet tall, their legs bent at an odd angle as they stalked forward. They each held a thick chain that had been wound around their inside wrists, the twin lengths leading back into the shadows. The Lycans had taken no more than a few steps when they jerked on the chains, and her brother appeared.

Bound like an animal.

Biting at her trembling lower lip, she glanced left, then right, surprised to see that others had joined her. Now the Bloodrunners and their family and friends stood as a united force against the Silvercrest pack, which had yet to accept the fact that something sinister was eating away at its foundation—something that would rip down the protective walls that separated their world from the humans'. It occurred to Michaela that loyalties were being announced tonight—a separation made between those who would stand with the Runners in their fight against the rogues and those who blindly supported the pack's refusal to face reality. But all she could focus on was her brother. Max looked so hurt…so terrified.

"Leave him alone," she screamed, her soft-soled, black satin slip-ons struggling for purchase in the damp earth as she rushed toward Max, only to find herself lifted off the ground when a hard, heavily muscled arm clamped around her waist from behind, pulling her clear off her feet. "Damn it, let me down!" she snarled, unable to take her eyes off her brother as the golden-eyed Lycan kicked him.

Mindless with heartache and rage, Michaela clawed at the arm holding her, kicking her heels against whatever part of her captor's legs she could reach. "Stop it," a deep, husky voice grunted in her ear. "You're not helping him by losing it. I give you my word he'll survive the ceremony, but you have to keep it together."

"Nooooo!" she screamed, too hysterical to listen to reason. "You're monsters! All of you! Look what you've done to him! How dare you! *How dare you!*"

The arm tightened with a powerful flex of muscle, cinching her waist. Her breath sucked in on a sharp, wailing gasp.

"Shut up before you get both yourself and your brother killed. I will *not* let that happen. Do you understand me?" her captor growled, shaking her so hard that her teeth clicked together. "Do you understand me, Doucet?"

"Damn it," she cried, stricken as she watched one of the guards grab Max by his hair. Around them Lycans huffed and growled as they watched the spectacle, while others outright howled for the show to begin.

"That's enough!" the voice seethed in her ear. "They'll tear you apart before you even reach him, and I'll be damned if I'm going to stand here and watch you die."

Suddenly, through the haze of fear and agony and outrage in her mind, she finally recognized who'd caught her. *Brody.*

He held her in his arms, her body locked against his powerful form, her back to the burning heat of his chest. A low, keening sound of anguish tore through her, and her

head dropped forward as hoarse sobs of pain ripped from
her throat. "Let me go. I have to help him. *Please,*" she
begged brokenly, knowing only that she needed to get to
Max. "Let me go, Brody."

He muttered something against her hair, his breath
warm against her scalp, and Michaela could have sworn it
was a single word.... But she must have heard wrong. She
was too upset. Too furious. Too terrified. She must be out
of her mind.

Because it sounded as if he'd quietly snarled the word
never.

HARLEQUIN® *Romance*®

Western Weddings

Jason Welborn was convinced that his business partner's daughter, Jenny, had come to claim her share in the business. But Jenny seemed determined to win him over, and the more he tried to push her away, the more feisty Jenny's response. Slowly but surely she was starting to get under Jason's skin....

Look for

Coming Home to the Cattleman

by

JUDY CHRISTENBERRY

Available May wherever you buy books.

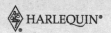

INTRIGUE

Introducing

THE CURSE OF RAVEN'S CLIFF

A quaint seaside village's most chilling secrets are revealed for the first time in this new continuity!

Britta Jackobson disappeared from the witness protection program without a trace. But could Ryan Burton return Britta to safety—when the most dangerous thing in her life was him?

Look for

WITH THE MATERIAL WITNESS IN THE SAFEHOUSE

by CARLA CASSIDY

Available May 2008 wherever you buy books.

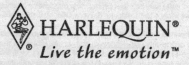

HARLEQUIN®
Live the emotion™

REQUEST YOUR FREE BOOKS!

2 FREE NOVELS PLUS 2 FREE GIFTS!

Passionate, Powerful, Provocative!

SDES08

SPECIAL EDITION™

 THE WILDER FAMILY
Healing Hearts in Walnut River

Social worker Isobel Suarez was proud to
work at Walnut River General Hospital, so
when Neil Kane showed up from the attorney
general's office to investigate insurance fraud,
she was up in arms. Until she melted in his
arms, and things got very tricky...

Look for

HER MR. RIGHT?

by

KAREN ROSE SMITH

Available May wherever books are sold.

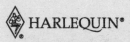

HARLEQUIN®

American ★ Romance®

Three Boys and a Baby

When Ella Garvey's eight-year-old twins and
their best friend, Dillon, discover an abandoned
baby girl, they fear she will be put in jail—
or worse! They decide to take matters into their
own hands and run away. Luckily the outlaws are
found quickly…and Ella finds a second chance
at love—with Dillon's dad, Jackson.

LOOK FOR

Three Boys and a Baby

BY

Laura Marie Altom

Available May
wherever you buy books.

LOVE, HOME & HAPPINESS

HARLEQUIN *Presents*

Don't forget Harlequin Presents EXTRA
now brings you a powerful new collection
every month featuring four books!

Be sure not to miss any of the titles in
In the Greek Tycoon's Bed,
available May 13:

THE GREEK'S
FORBIDDEN BRIDE
by Cathy Williams

THE GREEK TYCOON'S
UNEXPECTED WIFE
by Annie West

THE GREEK TYCOON'S
VIRGIN MISTRESS
by Chantelle Shaw

THE GIANNAKIS BRIDE
by Catherine Spencer

COMING NEXT MONTH

#1867 BOARDROOMS & A BILLIONAIRE HEIR—Paula Roe
Diamonds Down Under
She'd been blackmailed into spying on Sydney's most infamous corporate raider. Until he turned the tables and seduced her into a marriage of convenience.

#1868 FALLING FOR KING'S FORTUNE—Maureen Child
Kings of California
This millionaire playboy was about to enter a loveless marriage sure to make his wallet bigger...until a woman he'd never met claimed to be the mother of his child.

#1869 MISTRESS FOR A MONTH—Ann Major
He will stop at nothing to get her inheritance. But her price is for her to become his mistress...for a month.

#1870 DANTE'S STOLEN WIFE—Day Leclaire
The Dante Legacy
The curse of *The Inferno* left this billionaire determined to make her his bride...and he doesn't care that she's his own twin brother's fiancée.

#1871 SHATTERED BY THE CEO—Emilie Rose
The Payback Affairs
To fulfill the terms of his father's will, a business tycoon must convince his former love to work for his company—and try to find a way to stay out of her bed.

#1872 THE DESERT LORD'S BABY—Olivia Gates
Throne of Judar
He must marry and produce an heir if he is to become king. But he doesn't know his ex-lover has already given birth to his child....

SDCNM10408